I0675172

OATHBREAKER

GAMEBREAKERS #5

ELISE FABER

KAT MIZERA

GAMEBREAKERS

ONE

BRIAR

"Colt!"

I can't possibly be seeing what I'm seeing.

Colt died five years ago.

He *died*.

Hell, I'm standing right next to his headstone, his name engraved in the marble.

And yet...he's walking out of the shadows. No—

He's *limping* out of the shadows, slowly making his way toward me.

It's that slow, pained gait that finally snaps me out of my shock, has me believing the improbability of what I'm seeing. If this was a fantasy—and I've had plenty of them about Colt—he would be striding over the rolling hills, shirt unbuttoned, coat open and flowing, a la Mr. Darcy, searching for me, worried for me...

And declaring, "You must know...surely you must know it was all for you."

But he's not.

He's maneuvered his way out from the shadows and into the

moonlight, and while he's moving steadily, it's not the poignant ending of a romantic film.

Because he's moving painfully.

So damned painfully.

"Colt," I say again, staring in his direction, and I know he hears me this time because his gaze locks on to mine, mouth hitching up at one corner, giving me The Smile.

The one that had me falling in love with him the first time Dash brought him home from college break.

To give him a place to crash for a few weeks while school was out of session.

Because Colt's family...

Well, suffice to say, for as much as my parents are involved in their own lives and not super interested in what my brother and I are doing with ours (and they've been that way from the moment we hit our teenaged years), Colt's parents make ours look like Mom and Dad of the Year.

My heart warms at the memory because, God, Colt was such a fish out of water those first few days. Then he settled in, and I got to see his wicked sense of humor, that smile.

Add in a handsome package, a body a teenaged girl dreams of, and a sweet, protective streak a mile wide...

There was never anything for me to do except fall.

And I did it hard.

We close the distance between us, and I get my first good look at him.

"Oh, my God!" I gasp.

He looks terrible, and I don't mean that in the whole he-didn't-sleep-well-last-night sort of way. I mean that he looks *terrible*—he's skinnier than I've ever seen him, having lost well over thirty pounds, and he's covered in cuts and bruises. They line his arms, cut upon cut, some stitched up, some worse than that, I presume, since there are bandages covering them.

And the bruises.

God, the bruises.

They're a rainbow of yellows and blues, of greens and purples and almost blacks.

They disappear beneath the sleeves of his shirt, but start right back up again on his throat, spread over his face.

A new scar on his cheek, bisecting his eyebrow, an ugly red one disappearing into his hair.

Which is longer than I've ever seen it—months and months beyond the required military closely cropped cut.

"You're hurt," I whisper, worry rippling through me.

"I'm okay," he says, drawing to a halt, close enough that I can see that for the lie it is.

Agony clings to the edges of his expression, shadows his eyes, hangs off his far too skinny frame.

Hell, it seems a wonder that he's standing at all.

Then I process that this man—the one we all thought was dead for *five* fucking years—is standing in front of me.

Swaying in front of me.

I reach for him. "I—"

Before I can take his hand—or catch his shoulder to steady him—he's moving, wrapping me in his arms, holding me tightly against him.

And for a second, my worry disappears.

For a second, I'm lost in the feeling of Colt holding me, of Colt being here, of Colt being *alive.*

"It's so good to see you, baby," he rasps.

My lungs hitch. "I-I've missed you so much. We all have."

"Damn right you have," he quips, cocky entering his tone full-on.

Which is the moment that all of those good feelings turning my insides to goo go by the wayside, drifting away right alongside the worry.

Yes, his arms around me feel good, feel right, feel *exactly* like I remember.

But the man hugging me is supposed to be dead.

D.E.A.D.

And yet, he's standing here, holding me, arms wrapped tightly around me, fingers drifting down toward my ass—

Drifting *over* the curve of my ass.

"Little Briar Dash is all grown up," he teases, cupping the curve—which is, yes, larger than the last time he saw me. A product of life and pregnancy and five long years.

I choke—on my shock, my hurt...

My anger.

So, when he pulls back slightly and tugs at a lock of my hair, smiling The Smile at me, cockiness all up in his face, I don't melt like I once did.

I yank myself out of his hold. "You're supposed to be dead," I accuse.

He leans slightly to the side and pauses, pain spreading through his expression, but clearly, his wicked sense of humor is intact because he says, "I'd have to be dead to not appreciate that ass."

"Colt," I grind out.

He winks, eyes drifting to my chest. "And those breasts." A low groan. "Christ, Briar, but you're fucking gorgeous."

My lungs freeze.

Then my temper snaps.

I step forward and slap him across the cheek, the *crack* sounding loudly through the air.

"How dare you?" I whisper, tears flooding my eyes, clinging to my lashes. "How *dare* you after all this time just show up and say that and—" My throat closes, tears streaming down my cheeks. "Y-you were dead and—"

He reaches for me.

But I'm already reaching for him, throwing my arms around his neck, launching myself at him, hugging him.

Too tightly, considering his grunt.

Or maybe that was the whole *launching myself at him* part.

Either way, he's in my arms and he's hugging me back, and the bevy of emotions—disbelief, confusion, shock, hurt, anger...and biggest, because of course it's the biggest, is relief.

He's here.

He's *alive.*

After I finally let him go.

My lungs hitch and my eyes burn with tears all over again.

I have so many questions for him, so many answers I want to demand from him...but tonight, with feet on his grave, my arms around his neck, I just...can't.

So, when he says, "I need to explain," I shift out of his hold and shake my head.

"Not tonight," I whisper.

He's hurt and barely standing.

My mind is so fucking twisted up I can barely find his hand and lace our fingers together.

"But the guys," he says. "And you. I—"

I squeeze his hand. "Colt," I begin, starting to draw him toward my car, his exhaustion flowing off him and rippling through the air. "Please," I say. "Please let's not do this tonight."

I lost him, this man I loved...

And he's here.

I mourned him for years...

And he's here.

I finally let him go...

And he's here.

I can't do this, can't face this, can't *handle* this.

Well, I can.

And I will.

Just...not tonight.

"But—"

"I'm not ready for this tonight." I turn to him, eyes burning into his. "So, for me?" I whisper, watching his face change, his expression soften. "Please, just not now."

His chest lifts and falls on a breath that has him wincing.

Then he tables the pain.

And nods.

Relief slides through me—Frankie and West and the past and the present and him being here now...

Not tonight.

Tomorrow, I'll brace.

Tomorrow, I'll be ready.

Tomorrow, I'll face this.

But tonight—

"Thank you," I whisper.

"Anything for you, baby."

More guilt, more confusion, more *anger*...but I shove that all down too.

Because...*not tonight.*

I open the door of my car, help him into the passenger's seat, and buckle him in before rounding the hood and doing the same with myself in the driver's seat.

It's only when I'm driving out of the cemetery that I ask,

"Where's home for you?"

Two

COLT

Pain.

It's all I've known for four long years and today is no different.

Maybe a little different.

Instead of pain drowned out by fear, today it's just... an ache. Discomfort. A soreness that transcends everyday life. But the bed I'm in is soft and the blanket covering me is warm, which is a step in the right direction. Not like the last four years.

The cold was numbing.

The growls of hunger from my stomach were sometimes louder than my screams during the beatings. Somehow, the pain was always overshadowed by fear. Not of what else they were going to do to me—my training prepared me for that—but of what I was going to miss.

Fear that I wouldn't live to fight another day.

Fear that I'd never see my brothers again.

Fear that my sacrifice would be for naught.

Fear that I'd never get a chance to tell the woman I loved how I felt about her.

And last night I followed her to a cemetery where she was kneeling in front of my fucking grave before I stepped out of the trees and scared the crap out of her.

My beautiful Briar.

The thought of coming back to her is the only reason I'm still alive. The reason I continued to push through when it would have been so much easier to give up, let them kill me.

A brisk knock at the door startles me fully awake and I sit up in confusion. Then the door opens and—Briar.

Fuck, she's a breath of fresh air, the brightest sunshine of summer, and beauty personified. If I could bottle her up, I'd never work another day in my life. That might be corny, but it's true.

"Good morning." She steps inside briskly, letting the door click closed behind her. She's carrying two big shopping bags, and the scent of coffee and something slightly sweet hits my nostrils.

"If you brought breakfast, I might kiss you."

She arches a brow. "You're in no condition to be kissing anyone. Lay down and let me look at your bruises."

Who am I to say no when the love of my life asks me to lie down in bed?

"Christ, Colt, what happened?" Her eyes are sharp, fingers light, touch warm as she runs her fingers over my torso.

"It's a long story, babe."

She flinches—almost like I hit her—and regret settles over me like a dark, heavy blanket.

I have so much explaining to do, I don't know where to start.

"I'm not going anywhere," she says finally.

Yeah, my girl is upset.

I'd be worried if she wasn't.

I'm just not sure how to explain the massive clusterfuck I created.

"How far back should I go?" I ask after a moment.

"Uh, how about the beginning?" she snips, dabbing a cotton ball of something that burns like hell on one of the open sores on my chest.

"Well, the basic story is that I didn't re-enlist—I was recruited to a Black Ops unit. It's not officially part of any agency. Or the Marines. That's all I can tell you for security reasons."

"You became...a spy?" she asks, her eyes snapping to mine.

I nod.

It's close enough. There are other terms we used, but they don't matter. None of it matters to me anymore.

The salve she rubs on one of my bruises is cool and soothing, and the moan that escapes me is inadvertent. My eyes close, and I just lie there as she rubs a little more on my shoulder, the underside of my jaw, my forearm. Eventually she stops, and I realize she's waiting.

Fuck, but this is hard.

"So, when I left you, I went dark for a year. Complete immersion in hardcore training. All the things you see on TV times a million. Navy SEAL training combined with MMA fighting, foreign language studies—it was the most intense thing I could've imagined." I pause. "They didn't tell me ahead of time that it would be a complete blackout, no contact with the outside world at all. I didn't know, Briar. Every night in my bunk I wrote you letters and—"

"You did not." Her face is steely.

I take a breath. "I did. I know now that they never sent them, but I wrote them." I pause. "I also had no idea they...killed me off."

This time she sucks in a breath, her eyes fixed on mine. "You didn't...know?"

I shake my head. "When they sent me out on my first mission it was supposed to be simple: Get arrested in Siberia, find the agent who was already imprisoned in the prison there, and break us both out. We had people on the outside waiting, so it should have been a quick in and out."

She's stopped moving. I don't even know if she's breathing, she's staring at me so intently.

"And then it all went wrong. Our agent was already dead, and when they got wind of the questions I was asking in trying to find him..." I let her use her imagination.

"You were captured."

"Well, I was already in prison. But instead of spending thirty days for being a careless American who did something stupid, they figured out I was a...spy. And everything changed."

Her eyes get cloudy and then she abruptly turns away. "I have breakfast. Do you still like your coffee with sugar?"

She remembers.

"Yes. Thank you." I take the proffered cup.

"And chocolate croissants."

God, I love this woman.

"Perfect."

She busies herself putting croissants on plates, digging out napkins and arranging our breakfast for us. "Eat the sandwich first," she says, thrusting a bagel with what looks like bacon, egg and cheese at me. "You need protein. The croissant is dessert."

I take the first bite staring into her gorgeous green eyes.

She's even more beautiful now that she's older. Emerald-green eyes, ivory skin, and fiery-red hair that matches her some-times explosive personality. It's one of my favorite things about her.

"What?" she asks, scowling when she catches me smiling at her.

"I'm enjoying my sandwich—and the view."

Her cheeks flush pink and she dips her head. "Don't say things like that."

"Why not?"

"It's been five years, Colt!" There's that temper I love so much. "This isn't like you were deployed for six months. We buried you. We mourned you. We lost you. _I_...lost you." A single tear rolls down her cheek and she swipes at it angrily, another wave of guilt hitting me right in the gut.

I didn't know what the powers that be were doing in the background. I was focused on the mission. And getting back to my girl. I figured with a year's worth of salary building up while I was in training, I could buy her a ring when I got home.

Once she started receiving my letters, she'd understand.

She would *wait*.

Except those letters were never sent and... the painful reality hits me that Briar didn't wait. She had nothing to wait for.

I was dead.

For nearly five long years she believed I was dead.

Fuck. Me.

"Babe, I—"

Her phone buzzes, and she whips it out of her pocket.

"I'm sorry, I have to take this." She answers in a cool, professional voice I've never heard before. "What's going on?" She listens. Annoyance crosses her features. "Are you kidding me? Now?" More silence, and it ticks me off that I can't hear the other end of the conversation even though it has nothing to do with me. "Yes, I'm coming. I'm on the other side of town, though, so it'll probably take me an hour in traffic... Yup. I'm on my way." She stuffs the phone back in her pocket. "I have to go. I'm sorry. There's an issue at the office."

I don't know exactly what she does for work, but I know she works for my friend Atlas Delarosa. Who has apparently become one of the richest men in the world in the last five years. I assumed she was his secretary or some kind of executive assistant, but the tension in her face and her body language tell me she's more. A lot more.

And I'm dying to know how much.

Are they together?

I can't even fathom it.

Atlas would never touch his buddy's little sister.

Unlike me.

"Are you coming back?" I ask finally, practically holding my breath as I wait for her response.

She doesn't disappoint.

Her brows rise up toward her hairline as she snaps, "What the fuck are you talking about? Of course I'm coming back! You think I'm letting you disappear again?"

I almost smile.

Almost.

I sense she won't take kindly to jokes right now, so I have to be careful.

She's upset—and it has nothing to do with work.

"I'm not going anywhere, Thorny." The old nickname slips off my tongue easily and it has the expected reaction: Aggravation.

Good.

I'd rather she be mad than resigned or indifferent.

If she's mad, she still cares.

And that's the most I can hope for.

Somehow, I have to dig myself out of the nightmare my life has become and find my way back to my family.

THREE

BRIAR

My eyes are burning.

Then again, not sleeping after finding out my dead lover is actually alive after all these years will do that to a girl.

I'm so glad Royal and Jade promised to spend the day with Frankie today.

I don't think I would have had it in me to keep up the charade all day.

We're all a little subdued after Colt's birthday, so the dark circles upon dark circles beneath my eyes can definitely be explained away by the heavy emotions and killer hangover.

But that fades as the day goes on.

Because *life* goes on.

Trying to hide the fact that Colt is alive and I didn't immediately tell everyone...well, that's not going to be a fun conversation.

I sigh.

I don't even know why I didn't immediately call Dash.

Yes, he's injured. Yes, I was shocked.

But...I sigh again as I pull into the parking lot.

I wanted just a little bit of time with Colt that wasn't taken up by everyone else, that didn't leave me on the sidelines with a complicated knot of feelings, a heavy dose of uncertainty (and insecurity) as I watched.

Because I've spent a lot of my time watching my life go by.

Back then.

And now.

So, maybe it was wrong, *likely* it was wrong. But Colt and I need to talk. I have things I need to explain—so many things—and he needs to heal. Because he's in absolutely no shape to face the Gamebreakers.

They'll chew him up and spit him out.

He needs time to rest up, for those bruises to fade.

We need time to talk.

Then he can tackle handling the guys.

That's not what they would want, but they're just going to have to deal.

I park in my spot—one of the perks of working for the big man is that I have a designated parking space (it even has a sign with my name on it) right by the entrance of the building.

Initially, this was because I was hauling Frankie into the office with me and those car seats are no joke when it comes to loading and unloading from the back of a beat-up sedan and hauling them up to the top floor of a skyscraper—especially when a woman makes chonky babies.

Back then my arm muscles were on point.

As was my cardio.

And eventually, the spot became something I've earned.

Something I've worked hard for.

Something that's landed me in the office on a Saturday.

Sighing—because that seems to be my M.O. for the day—I snag my purse and haul my butt out of my midsized SUV (all the better for hauling Frankie and her friends, and all the gear kids require, around), and badge into the building.

Badging again to get up to the executive floor.

Fancy, huh?

One would think so...except circling back to the whole working on a Saturday thing.

Atlas is already there by the time the elevator doors open up and spit me out in front of the glass-enclosed offices. He's in a white button down and slacks, the only accommodation to being here to put out corporate fires on a Saturday the fact that his sleeves are rolled up and he's not wearing a suit jacket. The jacket is likely tossed over the back of his chair.

The sleeves are either Lily's doing...

Or because he's frustrated and ready to kick some ass.

Maybe both.

"That good, huh?" I ask as he storms toward me, scowl upon scowl marring his handsome face.

Said scowl deepens. "I don't get enough time with Lily as it is, and now I have to come in on one of the few fucking days I have with her, and all because of a fucking container ship going awry and shareholders getting antsy."

I step close to him, loop my arm through his, and start guiding him back to his office where I know the team from all over the globe is on video call as we all frantically work to fix this...and settle the tetchy shareholder. "You know I can handle this."

He keeps scowling—and this time it's directed down at me. "I know you can. But if we both tackle this shit, we'll figure it out and both be home sooner."

He's not wrong.

However, I also know that Lily is flying out tomorrow.

And that he's right—he and Lily don't get enough time together as it is.

"True," I say as we walk.

But I don't get more than that out because he's drawing me to a halt, reaching out his free, and turning my face up to his.

He swipes his thumb beneath each of my eyes. "You're tired."

I shrug, try to make light of what last night was and what it meant...and what it turned into, even though Atlas doesn't know it yet.

"Too many Gamebreakers and too late of a night for this mama." I start forward again. "I'm better when I'm in bed by nine with the latest serial killer documentary."

And not tending the wounds of the man I fell in love with as a teenager who mysteriously reappeared from the dead.

Thankfully, my reply has the intended effect, and he chuckles.

We've made it into the office and my lips twitch when I see I called it. His suit jacket is hanging on the back of his chair...and all the monitors are on with the team working from multiple locations around the world.

I unloop my arm, move to the chair, and snag the coat.

Then as much as I want to take him up on his offer of finishing this shit sooner so I can finish dealing with *my* shit, I move back to him and snag his arm again, shove the coat into his arms. "Go home to Lily. Soak in your time with her while I handle this."

He starts shaking his head, but I see how torn he is, know I'll be able to nudge him back to his woman. "You need to get back to Frankie, too. I'll stay."

Now it's my turn to scowl. "Royal and Jade have her. I'm sure they'll be happy to keep her overnight too." I pull out my cell, intending to ask them to do just that. "And if not, Dash and Willow have been asking for Frankie time."

He exhales, considering. "Are you sure?" he asks.

"Well, if it goes *really* long, I may ask you for Monday off and I know how much you hate Mondays."

"Thorny," he warns.

Which reminds me of Colt, of the slightly raspy way he teased me with the nickname.

I shove that down, focus.

Both because I don't need Atlas to know something this big is up, and also because...because at some point, I'll need to get back to Colt, so I need to get this shit done.

"Go," I order, shooing him out the door, walking him back to the elevator, making sure he doesn't change his mind on the journey.

He's stubborn, this man.

And he's protective.

And he would put me first in an instant—not that I'm going to let him.

The elevator door opens with a ding, and he steps on. "Don't forget to call West. Maybe he can bring you dinner here if you're still working and you guys miss your reservation."

Reservation.

Dinner.

West.

I still, horror slicing through me as I remember.

I'm supposed to have a date tonight.

"Briar?" Atlas calls, worry creeping into his expression.

I slap a smile on my face. "If we miss our reservation, then I'm calling you and *you* can have dinner delivered for us."

The doors close, but not before I see him shake his head, lips curving up.

I know he'll do it.

Because he's Atlas.

But I can't sit in the blip of amusement at whatever meal my over-the-top, secret-romantic-at-heart big brother would cook up for West and me if I had to work late.

Because I'm too busy feeling guilty.

Because...West.

I'd forgotten all about West.

Four

COLT

Sleep comes easy, just not for long periods of time.

Nightmares are part of it. Discomfort is the rest.

Aside from the normal beatings, which were almost daily, there was a new guard toward the end and he hated me. Hated all Americans, really. Wanted me dead. And did his level best to make it happen without being too obvious.

My broken sternum and bruised kidney can attest to that.

When Igor finally got me out, he had to take me to a tiny hospital in Alaska until my superiors could bring me to D.C. for better care and debriefing.

I barely remember those first few days when I'm awake.

But in my dreams, it's all pretty vivid.

Gunshots ringing out when we finally got through the gate.

The bitter cold.

And the pain.

So much goddamn pain.

The now familiar stitch in my side screams for mercy as I drag myself to the bathroom.

I take care of business and then wash up, resting my hands on the cabinet so I can rest before making that walk back into the main room. Then I look in the mirror. Big mistake.

Who the fuck is this ugly bastard staring back at me?

Hair too long, bruises all over my face, and a bump on my nose that will require surgery to fix, they broke it that many times.

Fuck.

I'm desperate for a shower but don't think I can manage it now.

It's a good thing, too, because I've just gotten back in bed when there's a knock on the door and Briar steps in.

She looks almost as bad as I do. Okay, not really, but the dark circles under her eyes weren't there two days ago, and her expression is shrouded—like she's carrying the weight of the world on her shoulders. And I hate myself a little knowing it's because of me.

Stepping out of the shadows like I did probably wasn't the best move, but I wasn't brave enough—or physically strong enough—to get into the Sapphire Room. I followed Banks first because he was the easiest to find. Badass hockey player living in a big house—with a wife or live-in girlfriend and...a baby.

Watching him carrying in that car seat was jarring—because in my mind it's still five years ago. *My* life is picking up where it left off. The hard part is going to be understanding that everyone else's moved on.

This isn't the time to think about all that.

"When was the last time you slept?" I demand, forcing myself into a sitting position.

She knits her brows together, giving me a pointed look. "Don't worry about me. You're the one who's hurt—are you bleeding again? Where are you bleeding? Sit up, let me see."

I didn't even notice the blood on the sheets and try to twist to get a look at the bandage from my kidney surgery, but it hurts too much.

"I said, let me see." Firm fingers on my shoulder, holding me upright as she checks the wound. "This is opening, Colt. What have you been doing?"

"I thrash in my sleep," I admit. "Nightmares and shit. They wake me up."

Her eyes find mine worriedly. "Do you need—"

"What I need is to see Dash and the others, explain and—"

"You're in no position to see anyone. They're going to kick your ass when they find out you're alive." Her hands are on her hips now. "The best thing for you would be to come home with me."

"You, uh, live on your own?" I'm almost afraid to ask.

She scowls. "What kind of question is that? I'm not in college anymore. I have a job, responsibilities, a *life*. There have been a lot of changes since you've been gone... things you don't know."

That stings a little, but I nod. "Then tell me."

"We will, but first we have to come up with a plan to break the news to the boys because this is going to hit everyone hard. And somewhere in there, you're going to have to tell me how you came to be at the cemetery when I was there." Big green eyes burn with intensity and curiosity, and probably a touch of annoyance.

"I was following you," I say blandly. "How else?"

It's almost comical, the way I can see how much restraint it requires for her not to lose her temper.

That's my girl, the fiery redhead I fell in love with. Long before I was willing to give those feelings a name.

"Let's pack up your stuff." She looks around. "Is this all you have?"

"My entire life reduced to one duffel," I admit with a lopsided grin. "It makes packing and moving a cinch."

She purses her lips. "It's not funny, Colt."

I sigh. "I know, baby. But all I can do is crack a few jokes and try my best not to dwell on the last four years."

Her expression softens but she quickly turns away, pulling clothes out for me. "Sweats, okay? I think those will be easiest for you."

"Yeah. Thanks." I'd like to say I yanked them on and dressed myself, but the bleeding must be indicative of an infection or something because I'm weaker than I was a couple of days ago. So, standing up to put on my damn pants is apparently beyond the realm of my current capabilities.

"You need help." It's not a question, really.

My girl kneels in front of me, gently putting my feet into the sweat pants, lifting them to my knees, and then offering me her shoulder as I stand so she can support me as I pull them up.

This isn't how I pictured our reunion.

And it pisses me off.

"Thanks," I say quietly, at least managing to pull a T-shirt over my head.

"Do you have things in the bathroom?"

"Just a toothbrush, toothpaste, and deodorant."

"Let me grab those."

She bustles around doing everything except looking at me, and I desperately want to ask what she's thinking. Feeling. She's upset with me, and I can't blame her. But how will we get past this if we don't talk?

"Briar, I want to tell you—"

"Not now." She shakes her head, still not looking at me. "Please. Let me get you settled at the house and then see if we need to call in a doctor. Or take you to the E.R."

"I'll be okay," I say. "I pulled something when I was in Nashville and—"

"You were in Nashville?" She frowns.

"I thought maybe I'd talk to Atlas first." This time I'm the one who looks away. "I chickened out. And also, I didn't realize it was a big, public funeral. I didn't want to do anything to interrupt that. It's a good thing, too, because I did rip out my stitches getting there, so I was back in the E.R. for a few days before I could fly to L.A."

A million emotions cross her face in that moment but then she just picks up my bag.

"Let me put these in the car. I'll be right back."

I hate feeling helpless. Nervous. Unsure of myself.

This isn't what I want but I keep reminding myself that it's been five long years since Briar saw me. She thought I was dead. That's the part that really guts me. What we shared right before I left goes a lot deeper than her virginity. That was the beautiful, meaningful cherry—no pun intended—on top of the sundae that represented the future we talked about.

I had to get through training. That much I told her. Then I would talk to Dash.

Well, I didn't tell her that.

We spent two days loving and dreaming and planning.

She'd work for a year while I figured out the next phase of my career. Then I'd come home and ask her to marry me.

I stupidly didn't tell her *that* either.

Instead, I wrote letters.

Letters she never got.

Mother. Fucker.

I get pissed off all over again when I think about the sheer arrogance of my superiors—making life-changing decisions without telling me.

It's easier, they told me during my debriefing. To let go of everything in your past. And so that there's no one they can use to manipulate you. No one they can torture you to get information about.

What they didn't understand is that I would have—and almost did—die before I told them about Briar or the boys. There was nothing they could do to me to get me to give up the only family I have.

The family—and woman—I may have lost now thanks to those damn decisions.

Some were my own, but the rest was all them.

And something scarier than the worst torture I endured?

Not knowing if I can fix this.

FIVE

BRIAR

"I'm sorry," I say and that's basically the only truth that's come out of my mouth during this entire conversation.

"Baby," West says, his voice a gentle rumble that I love. It's soothing. It's soft. It's kind. It makes me feel good—

Usually.

Today it's another slice of guilt.

Because I'm breaking our date to take care of Colt.

Because I'm lying to the man I was falling in love with, was planning on building a future with, was—

Was.

Fuck.

I close my eyes, fighting back my tears as another lash of guilt slices through me—and then deeper when I hear him go on.

"Our date will hold," he says. "The important thing right now is for you to get done what you need to get done so you can get some rest."

More guilt.

Sweet baby Jesus, this guilt is going to slice me into a thousand pieces.

"Thanks, West."

"Anytime, honey," he murmurs. "Now, go kick some ass in that meeting of yours. I can't wait to hear all about it."

Hear all about me lying to him about the shitshow I dealt with today running long?

Or hear all about the truth of what I've actually been doing over the last several hours—driving back over to Colt's hotel room, packing up his stuff and helping him out to my car. Then, considering his wound was still oozing blood, stopping by an urgent care and getting a doctor to look at his stitches. They'd fixed him up and by the time I got him back into my car, he was pale, trembling, and barely upright.

My heart had ached for him, for the suffering he so clearly endured, for what was clearly the hell of the last five years, for all that he'd been through while we were here building our lives without him—

"Briar?"

I blink and...more guilt.

Because even during a quick phone call to the man I'm supposed to be in love with, supposed to be taking the next step with...

I'm thinking about Colt.

It was bad enough when I was wrestling with what I'd lost, when I was trying to tamp down the promise of what we had, the yearning of what we *could* have had.

It's worse knowing that I drove Colt home from the urgent care and installed him in my guest bedroom.

Worse still knowing that I need to figure out the best way to break the news of his reappearance from the dead to my brothers...

To Frankie.

"Honey?"

West's tone is firmer, worry creeping in along the edges.

"I really am sorry," I whisper.

He sighs and I know that if he was here, he'd pull me into

his chest, would wrap his strong arms around me. I'd smell the spicy male scent of him, feel the steady warmth of him, would be able to relax and know that I was safe and content and *wanted*.

But he's not here.

And my life—and my *love* life—has gotten a lot more complicated.

So much more complicated.

"Do you want to sleep at my house?" he says. "Come over whenever you're done?"

God, no.

I can't have West and his strong arms and broad chest—not to mention his truly impressive kissing skills—muddle my head further.

I need to think.

I need to plan.

I need—

"It doesn't matter how late you'd be," he murmurs. "I'd just be happy to wake up next to you."

Because we haven't done that yet.

Because we haven't done *it* yet.

"I'm really tired," I reply back, my tone soft. "I should probably finish up and head home."

He's quiet for a moment. "Okay, sweetheart." Then before I can respond, he says, "I'll let you get back to it so you can get it done and get home."

Another lash of guilt.

"Thanks, West," I whisper.

"Text me when you get home."

"I will," I say, and I hate that it's another lie. I'll text him, of course I will.

But it'll be another lie because I'm going to set an alarm to text at a suitably late hour and pretend to just be arriving home and sliding into bed.

Ugh.

I shove that down and ignore the guilt battering at my insides as we say our goodbyes and hang up.

I set that alarm.

Pretype the text so I can just hit send later.

Then I gird my loins.

Because Colt is here.

He's alive.

And I need to talk to him about something important.

About something even more important than his reappearance from the other side.

Something that doesn't just affect me.

Exhaling, I head downstairs, turn the corner, and push into the guest room to find—

Colt asleep.

So heavily asleep that he doesn't shift in the least when I pad across the floor and sit on the edge of the bed, calling softly.

So deeply that he doesn't move when I gently shake his shoulder.

I bite back the urge—and no surprise the *guilt* that comes—to shake him awake.

I walk back out, quietly shut the door, and go back upstairs, intending to take a bath and catch up on the never-ending pile of laundry that all moms of small children have while watching something inane on TV.

But I don't make it that far.

I lay down—just for a few minutes.

And the next thing I know, the alarm is waking me.

I hit send, blearily poke my head in on Colt to find him still sleeping.

So, I give in to the fatigue, the weariness that's gnawing at my bones, and I go to bed.

I'll figure out how to tell everyone all the things I need to tell them in a few more hours.

Just a few more hours.

I lay down.

And let sleep come.

———

The next thing I'm aware of is voices.

Heart seizing, I jerk upright and realize that it's morning, that sun is shining through my windows.

That Royal and Jade must be here.

Bringing Frankie home.

Gasping, I launch myself out of bed and hurry down the stairs, intercepting them before they can get *anywhere* near the guest bedroom.

"Mom!" Frankie exclaims, rushing toward me and wrapping her arms tightly around my waist.

My heart spasms.

God, I love my girl.

"Hey, baby," I say, and I do it calmly even though my heart is threatening to pound its way out of my chest, keenly aware of the time bomb hopefully still sleeping in the guest room down the hall.

"Uncle Royal and Auntie Jade and I all wrote a song together. Do you want to hear it?"

I squeeze her tightly for a moment then push down my freak-out. "Absolutely," I tell her. "But you need to bring your things up to your room and put them away first."

Her bottom lip juts out, as though she's considering arguing that...and if she might win that argument.

I just lift my brows at her and wait.

She sighs, sticks out her bottom lip a teensy bit further, but to her credit, she drops her arms and goes and grabs her backpack from her Auntie Jade.

I watch her start up the stairs then whip around to face Royal and Jade.

"I need to talk to you."

He blinks, glances at Jade, whose eyes have gone wide with concern.

"Both of you," I say, knowing that my voice and manner aren't anywhere near the calm I affected for my daughter.

And knowing that if anyone has any chance of making it so that Royal won't lose his mind and beat up an already injured Colt, it's Jade.

Royal glances back at me. "Okay."

I nod, heart pounding even more intensely.

God, I was supposed to have time to plan, supposed to have time to know the right words to say to explain, supposed to—

I hear a thud from upstairs and know I'm out of time.

I need to explain, and I need to do it quickly.

"Kitchen," I say. "Now."

SIX

After four years in a Russian prison camp, I learned to sleep lightly and assess my surroundings before opening my eyes. Always. And based on the uneven breathing I hear, someone is hovering over the bed. Since I'm no longer in that prison camp, I'm not particularly worried, so I slowly pry my lids open.

There's a pair of cobalt blue eyes just inches from my face, staring at me intently.

The eyes belong to a little girl with wavy dark hair, and she doesn't seem to be at all uncomfortable watching a stranger sleep.

She's beautiful, no more than three or four years old, but I'm not sure what she's doing here at Briar's—

Briar's words from the other night suddenly come rushing back.

There have been a lot of changes since you've been gone... things you don't know.

Is this little girl one of those changes? One of the things I don't know?

Did one of the boys have a kid? I know Banks recently had a

baby–it was all over the sports pages I scoured–but this kid is too old for that. I can't picture Atlas or Dash having a kid, but Royal would... maybe. I probably shouldn't assume anything since I've been gone a long time.

Maybe this girl is–

"Are you my dad?" she asks, interrupting my rambling and probably incoherent thoughts.

I blink, caught off-guard.

"I...don't think so." I clear my throat, frowning. Taking in the shape of her face. Her eyes. Even her hair color...

It's not possible.

Is it?

"Then why is your picture in my room?" She puts a fist on her hip, narrows her eyes, and gives me a piercing look that's going to send little boys scrambling in the near future. "And why does Mommy cry when she sees it sometimes? And how come—"

"Okay, give me a second, kiddo. I just woke up." I rub my eyes and slowly try to stretch, see what hurts the most, and try not to aggravate it.

Mostly, I'm trying to buy myself some time to wrap my head around this little girl who has eyes... Just. Like. Mine. Cobalt blue with thick, dark lashes. In college, my teammates used to tease me about my lashes, asking what kind of mascara I use. It was funny then. Not so much now.

Looking at this kid is like staring into a mirror.

I think there's a picture somewhere of me at a similar age—in my storage unit maybe?—where we might be twins.

It's suddenly hard to breathe and myriad emotions rocket through me.

Guilt.

Shame.

Curiosity.

Excitement...

Do I have a kid?

"What's... your name?" I finally ask.

"Frankie." She cocks her head, like she's waiting for something.

But I'm finding it hard to breathe.

Her name is Frankie?!

My father's name was Frank. The only person who ever loved me. He was killed in Afghanistan after 9/11. And I told Briar all about him. This can't be a coincidence. I don't believe in them.

"What's your name?" she counters when I don't say anything.

"I'm...Colt." I don't know if I'm supposed to tell anyone who I am.

Briar was clear that we had to come up with a plan on how to announce that I was back from the dead, but it would be rude not to answer this adorable little girl who watches me like she knows all the secrets to my world.

"Colt. The guy my mommy used to love."

Oh, sweet Jesus.

I don't dare hope...do I?

"Aren't you dead?" she continues.

I almost laugh. What else can I do?

"I was... lost," I say after a moment. "In a place really far away. Everyone thought I died in an accident, but I didn't."

"Are you going to make mommy cry again?"

Not if I can help it.

Not if I can get her to forgive me.

Not if—enough!

I need information. Answers to questions I haven't had time to think of.

"How old are you?" I ask, trying to still the wild beating of my heart.

"Four and three-quarters." Her eyes are guileless as she watches me watching her.

"When's your birthday?"

"February twenty-first... when's yours?"

"October tenth," I reply automatically, but I can barely think.

Briar and I made love around the twentieth of May. If she'd

gotten pregnant, the baby would have come nine months later...
around the twenty-first of February.

Fuck.

Is it possible?

Did I leave Briar pregnant with my baby?

I pull in a shaky breath. This is unexpected and all the things I
was planning to say to her go right out the window.

If this is my daughter, that means I abandoned her when she
needed me most. How the hell do we come back from this? I
don't think there's a single thing I can do to make it up to her. To
either of them.

My stomach churns with guilt and fury. At all the bad luck.
Miscommunication, both on my part and that of my superiors. I
run my hands down my face to buy a little time. Try to breathe
through emotions that are hitting me so hard I feel a little
nauseated.

"Are you sick?" Frankie asks after a moment. "Should I go get
Mommy?"

"No. I'm okay." I stare at her. My daughter. She's my daughter. There is no doubt in my mind.

"You don't look okay. Your face looks funny." She reaches out
a tiny finger, gently running it over my right eye. That's one of the
worst bruises, and it's still a kaleidoscope of colors as it heals.
"Does your booboo hurt?"

"A little."

"Did you fall off your bike?"

I smile, shaking my head. "No. I was in a different kind of
accident and needed an operation. But I'm getting better."

"My mommy is really good at making people feel better.
Whenever my tummy hurts, Mommy rubs it and lets me cuddle
with her. Then like magic, it goes away."

I can't help but smile even though part of me wants to cry.

I have no doubt that Briar is a good mom.

Even if the man she thought she was going to have a future
with abandoned her, she wouldn't have let that stop her from

doing whatever she had to do to make her child's life safe and happy.

She must have been so damn hurt that she couldn't reach me. And then, adding insult to injury, the organization I work for decided to tell the world—my family and the woman I love—that I was dead.

Horror washes over me.

If I were Briar, I would hate me.

What fresh hell is this?

I thought I'd reached rock bottom those last weeks in Siberia, when the cold and starvation and ongoing torture seemed to have gotten the best of me. I was ready to die, to let go of the pain and humiliation, and succumb to the darkness. As far as I was concerned, there had been nothing left to fight for.

It would have been completely different if I'd known I had a kid. That Briar had—No. I have to stop. There's no reason to believe this little girl is mine. Pregnancy isn't exactly nine months. She probably went out and fucked me right out of her system with guys who were going to stay around.

Except... as far as I can tell, she's single. And anyway, I know Briar wouldn't do that. The sweet, innocent woman who gave me her virginity and told me she'd loved me for a long time? The one who laid in my arms and planned a future with me? No, she didn't fuck other guys right away. Probably not for a long time.

And no matter how many excuses I can think up, the truth is staring at me in a compact, sturdy little body. With my eyes. My nose. Even her eyebrows are the same shape as mine. Jesus.

"Where's your mommy?" I ask Frankie.

"In the kitchen with Uncle Royal and Auntie Jade."

Royal.

He's right here in the house with me, basically just steps away.

I have to see him, talk to him—explain.

There are voices down the hall that are getting louder and I'm just about to throw off the covers to go intervene when I remember I'm naked. I got up to go to the bathroom in the middle of the night and couldn't get my sweats back on, so I didn't bother.

I glance at Frankie. "You have to turn around, kiddo."

"How come?" She scrunches up her face and—she might look like me, but her expressions are one hundred percent Briar.

"I have to put some pants on."

SEVEN

BRIAR

"What's going on?" Royal asks as we move into the kitchen, Jade on our heels. "What's wrong?"

"I—" I shake my head.

Because how the hell do I begin?

Oh, by the way, the friend you thought was dead and gone is actually alive?

He's just bruised and battered and recovering right down the hall in my guest room.

I groan and scrub my fingers over my face.

"Thorny," he murmurs, voice gentling. "Talk to me."

"It's complicated," I say through my hands. Then exhale and drop them to my sides. "I'm not sure where to start."

He studies me then slants a look at Jade. "How about at the beginning?" she says gently, setting a foil-covered casserole dish on the counter.

"Right," I begin.

Then stop.

Because *a foil-covered casserole dish.*

Oh, my God.

It's Sunday.

Sunday dinner.

And Colt is in the guest room, and I didn't start anything for dinner—something that will immediately clue *everyone* in to the fact that something's up and seriously off and—

It's Sunday.

Sunday *dinner*.

Royal and Jade are the first to arrive.

But, yes, everyone else is coming.

"Oh, no," I whisper.

"Briar." Royal drops his hand onto my shoulder. "Stop freaking out and start talking."

"Before everyone gets here, I have to tell you something important. Something *really* important—"

But that's when I hear the front door open again.

"Where's my favorite sister?" Dash calls down the hall.

"Oh, my God."

This isn't going to plan.

This is...a disaster.

"She's our only sister, dumbass," I hear Banks say. Something that would normally make me feel all soft and squishy inside—because we're not blood, but we're bound more tightly than genetics could possibly make us.

"Language," Aspen says. "Because if Maisie's first word is dumbass or fuck or asshole, I will personally castrate all of you."

"Don't mention that she just said the top three," Atlas says dryly.

All of their voices are coming closer.

Lily's full-bodied laughter echoes our way.

Shit. *Shit.*

"Be nice," Willow chides gently.

Because she can be nothing but nice.

And then they're emerging into the kitchen, one after another, like they're exiting a clown car and tumbling out onto the street below, laughter and smiles abounding—first come

Banks and Aspen and Maise, then Atlas and Lily, then Hudson and Willow.

The conversation and teasing and banter continue.

For one more moment.

Because then they catch sight of me and Royal and Jade.

I'm sure my face is revealing far too much, and I saw the concern on Jade and Royal's faces—that can't be hard to miss either.

Atlas frowns, his mouth opening.

But Dash isn't thinking about his sister, isn't thinking about what no doubt must be pale skin and wide eyes and a jumpy as fuck demeanor.

He's thinking about his stomach.

And he speaks first, his eyes locking with mine.

"Are you not cooking?" he asks.

Nope. I haven't been thinking about dinner, haven't done anything except sleep the sleep of the dead and wake up to Frankie and co coming home and freaking out about the fact that *Colt is sleeping in my fucking guest room!*

"Um," I begin.

"Shit, Thorny," he mutters. "I'm hungry as fuck and a salad isn't going to fill me up."

"I brought a casserole," Jade says softly.

"Great," he says, still muttering.

Dash isn't a huge fan of casseroles—even the yummy ones that Jade makes.

"And I brought brownies," Aspen says.

"Better," my brother says.

"They're out of a box, but brownies are better than no brownies, am I right?"

"Atlas and I brought wine," Lily volunteers, shooting Jade a look. "For those of us who can drink."

Jade's cheeks go pink, but neither she nor Royal comment on Lily's probing.

"It's from Oak Ridge Vineyards, and it's delicious," Atlas

says, setting the bottles on the counter and then turning toward me, his expression full of concern. "Briar—"

"We brought some vegetable thing," Dash grumbles. "But again, that shit isn't going to fill me up."

"It's not shit!" Willow exclaims. "It's delicious and I worked hard to learn this recipe, Hudson!"

He wrinkles his nose. "It's only vegetables. Vegetables aren't a meal."

"I think vegetarians would disagree with that," Lily says dryly.

Dash rolls his eyes. "Well, clearly they've got a screw loose because they're not eating meat." A beat. "Which I need. Because I'm a growing boy."

Banks snorts and sets Maisie's car seat on the counter, starts unbuckling her. "So, Briar didn't cook for us. We'll order some pizzas. Meat lovers," he adds. "And anyway, leave our sister alone. She looks exhausted."

Aspen cocks her head to the side. "You're right. Briar *does* look exhausted."

Willow crosses over to me and takes my hand. "Are you feeling sick, honey? You should go lay down."

"Yes," Jade says. "We can feed Frankie and then get out of your hair."

"Is this like that time you got food poisoning in high school, and you spent forty-eight hours puking your guts up? *Ow!*" He glares at Atlas, who punched him hard in the chest.

"Stop being the annoying older brother and focus," he growls. "Briar isn't feeling well." His eyes come to mine. "I know I shouldn't have left you alone yesterday to deal with that shit. Dammit, you're pushing yourself too hard."

My temple throbs. "I'm fine—"

"You need to lie down," he says, moving straight into fix it mode. "Forget the pizzas. We're ordering chicken noodle soup and..." He snaps his fingers. "Saltines and ginger ale. That's like the trifecta of sick people food."

"And cold medicine," Banks says. "Oh, and Pepto, if she's got a tummy ache."

God, normally hearing the hot hockey star who is Banks talking about *tummy aches* would have cracked me up.

Tonight, I'm too stressed to enjoy the hilarity.

"Guys—"

"Did you and West have a fight?"

I glare at Lily as the air in the room goes taut. Christ, is there another question that could prickle *all* of their overprotective brotherly energy all at once? No. Absolutely not.

And worse?

Yes, there's a problem with West all right.

Mainly me forgetting he existed as I dealt with the man I used to love.

A man who's currently sleeping in the freaking *guest room!*

"Guys," I begin again.

"No," Banks says. "I saw West at practice this morning. He said that she"—a nod in my direction—"worked late but they were going to catch up when he comes over tonight."

First, comes the horror over the fact that Banks and West are talking about me.

At fucking Vipers' practice.

Next comes...he's *coming* over.

Because I invited West to Sunday Dinner.

Fuck. My. Life.

"Guys," I say for a third time. "I really need to—"

"Would he actually tell you if they were fighting though?" Dash mutters, immediately going from annoying and antagonizing to, well, still annoying, but now overprotective too.

"I—"

"Of course not," Atlas says, tapping at his phone. "I'll get my team to start an investigation. Find out what's really going on—"

Banks rolls his eyes. "West isn't like that. I told you—"

"I'll get his cell and email." Dash pulls out *his* phone. "You check in on his movements—"

Aspen's eyes are wide. "Boys, you should—"

Lily scowls at Atlas. "That's serious overkill—"

"It couldn't hurt," Royal begins.

Jade smacks him. "Don't encourage them."

"Hudson," Lily murmurs. "I think—"

And that's the moment the last of my control unravels.

"Just everyone fucking stop!" I shout, my head throbbing, my throat tight, my eyes dangerously close to tears.

Finally, there's silence.

Complete and total silence.

And that's followed quickly by even more concern.

Willow squeezes my hand. "Honey, what's wrong?"

My heart convulses.

God, I love these men and women. I love their concern, their protectiveness, the crazy, annoying banter.

I just...love them and the family we've built.

All of which means I have to level with them and I have to do it quick.

Only as I open my mouth to confess to the man currently in residence in my guest room, I see movement out of the corner of my eye.

Fuck.

Fuck!

Colt limps into the kitchen.

Then says, like the idiot he is—

"You didn't have to throw me a party."

EIGHT

COLT

Everyone in the room freezes to the point that it's almost comical. Like this is a movie and someone hit pause. But I'd been just outside the kitchen listening—to the banter, the laughter, Briar's discomfort. Her inability to get out the words.

And I had to save her.

Because this is all my fault and it's not fair for her to carry this burden for another minute. I can't imagine how hard it's been for her to keep this secret the last few days, so I did what I've always done—stepped up and made a joke.

Unfortunately, it fell flat.

Then someone I only know because I saw him kissing Briar the other night—and I still haven't decided if I'm going to kill him or not—slips in the back door, a look of concern on his face because—

The guys are staring at me like they've seen... well, a ghost. I'm supposed to be dead. Fuck, I feel like a real ass for that.

But it's Dash's expression that hits hardest.

Fury.

"Are you fucking kidding me?" he roars. He steps toward me, fists clenched, and Briar instinctively moves between us.

"Dash, no—he's hurt."

Then West pushes Briar behind him. Protecting her. Doing what I should be doing if I wasn't so fucking sore.

"Mommy?" Frankie's tiny voice, now filled with uncertainty, seems to break the daze everyone is in.

And like magic, the ladies spring into action.

"Frankie! Do you want to hear my new song?" Lily immediately holds out her hand. "If we go get your ukulele, I'll play it for you. Come on, show me where it is." She ushers Frankie out of the room, and I take a second to regroup.

This is my family, but I'm a stranger. A *dead* stranger. It's a really weird feeling and probably the worst situation I've ever been in.

Banks just looks confused, like he can't figure any of this out.

Royal seems more intrigued, like this is a puzzle for him to decode.

Atlas is mad, no doubt about that, his dark eyes nearly black as he studies me.

West looks like he wants to beat the crap out of me, which is equal parts funny and frustrating, because I don't know him and he doesn't know me. I'm also not sure I could take him in my current condition.

But it's Dash's expression that guts me.

He's so hurt that he wants to hurt *me* in return. Maybe not literally, but if Briar hadn't stepped in, he would've taken a swing. And I deserve that and much more.

The ladies are more reserved, trying to figure out who I am and what I'm doing here, as if I'm the stranger and not them.

That part hits me the hardest.

I've become a stranger in my own family. These women I don't know beyond what I could find online—*they're* part of the family now. And I'm the outsider.

The baby on the counter starts to whimper, and Aspen immediately reaches for her, lifting her into her arms and cooing softly. Banks is instantly at her side, one hand on his daughter's back, gently caressing.

"I'm going to take her outside." She looks at Banks and they exchange some mystical couple ESP that ends with him giving her a tiny nod. "Jade, you coming?"

"Uh, yeah." Jade nods after a similar exchange with Royal.

She grabs Willow's hand and the ladies, with the exception of Briar, make a hasty exit, leaving the rest of us standing in the kitchen, the air thick with tension.

"Motherfucker, you have a lot of explaining to do!" Dash growls, glaring at me.

"This isn't an episode of 'I Love Lucy,'" I joke, trying to lighten the mood the only way I know how. "You don't need to channel Desi and demand I do some 'splaining."

"You seriously think this is funny?" West grits out, scowling.

"You need to leave," I say dryly. "This has nothing to do with you."

"Yeah, good luck with that." West folds his arms across his chest, eyes narrowing, letting me know he's not going anywhere.

Fuck.

This isn't how I envisioned coming home. Seeing my friends.

I didn't want things to be so complicated. But for some reason, it never occurred to me the guys would be married, involved, having kids. I definitely never imagined that I had a kid. That Briar and I made a baby.

Jesus. Fucking. Christ.

"Well?" Dash makes a hurry up motion with his hands. "You going to stand there like a sad dipshit or are you going to fucking explain?"

"It's complicated," I respond slowly. "I was on a mission. Then I got captured." I glance at West. "Now I'm back."

"You came straight to L.A.?" Atlas asks.

"After being debriefed and spending a week in the hospital."

"Except you didn't," he says. "Because you were in Nashville, weren't you?"

Shit. I forgot about that.

"Yeah, but..." This is so difficult to explain. "I didn't realize what was going on until I got there. Once I figured out who Lily was, and it was the funeral for some big shot, I decided that wasn't the right place for us to talk. I thought I should wait until we were all together."

Atlas closes his eyes, his jaw working angrily, one fist clenched at his side. "You were in Nashville and didn't..." Voice tense, body coiled like he's ready to strike. "You know what? I'm out. Lily! Let's go!" He turns and storms out the door without looking back.

Dammit.

"Atlas..." I want to follow but I don't have the strength, and frankly, I don't know what I'd say. Sorry about all this? It's complicated...

"I didn't know you guys thought I was dead," I say, trying to regain some semblance of control. "I thought you'd be told that I was MIA or something, not dead. I wasn't allowed contact while I was in training and then—"

"Training." Dash meets my eyes, jutting out his jaw slowly. "You took that job with the black ops center. The one they told us about in that security meeting, where if we were interested to let our COs know." His face hardens. "We talked about it, you asshole. We decided, *together*, that neither of us was interested."

"I know." God, I hate this part. "But then they came to me separately, told me I had a specific skill set and that..." I drop my gaze, because this part is hard. "...I didn't have anyone waiting for me. No family to speak of. I was a perfect fit and—"

"No *family*?" Briar's voice is a hushed whisper filled with disbelief.

"You're serious." Dash opens his mouth and closes it again. "We—you know what? I can't do this right now." Dash holds up a hand stopping me from saying anything as he calls to his fiancée. "Babe? Willow, we're leaving."

And like Atlas, he doesn't wait for her, merely turns and walks out the door.

Good job, Colt. Alienating your brothers.

Exactly the homecoming you were counting on.

"He'll be back," Royal says after a moment. "He just needs a little time to digest it all. This probably hit him harder than the rest of us."

"Why?" I ask in confusion, even though I already know the answer.

Banks cocks his head, staring at me like I'm an idiot. "You know he blamed himself, right? He still thinks that if he'd re-enlisted with you, it might not have happened. That he should have been there—wherever you were when you died—and had your back. Like always."

Of course, Dash thought he could have prevented it. It would never cross his stubborn mind that he probably would have died *with* me, assuming we were on the same assignment.

Guilt and fury and shame course through my veins. "Fuck!"

I whirl, punching the wall with all the strength I have. The pain in my hand is intense enough to make me dizzy and I momentarily weave, needing to brace myself on the same wall I just tried to assault.

"Guys, please." Briar's voice is a whisper as she moves to my side, steadying me. "Can we all just go talk?"

"I don't think—" I cut myself off because I'm not ready to talk about the details of my decision back then. Certainly not in front of a stranger like West.

But I owe it to them.

Certainly to Briar.

Especially since I absolutely despise the way West is hovering, watching—like a man who's protecting his property. I can respect it, but I'll be damned if I'm not going to do everything in my power to make it stop.

Briar is mine.

Since the night she admitted she had feelings for me. The night she told me she wanted me to be her first, that she'd been waiting for me to make a move. When I didn't, she took matters into her own hands.

I fell in love with her then and I still love her now.

No way in hell I'm letting some playboy hockey stud take her.

Although, if possession is nine-tenths of the law, I'm screwed.

NINE

BRIAR

We've all shifted to the living room and take our seats. Or Colt, West, and I have sat, him in an armchair, me on the couch, West at my side, providing a human shield between me and my brothers.

"Dash wouldn't have hurt me," I say softly of him stepping in between us in the kitchen.

"He looked ready to commit murder," he says, no hint of apology in his words before his expression gentles and he cups my jaw. "I won't let anyone hurt you, baby. Not ever."

Unbidden, my eyes slide to the side and my heart thuds hard at the look in Colt's eyes.

Then West's fingers on my jaw flex and my gaze jerks back...

And guilt.

Because he saw me looking.

"West," I whisper.

"Later," he murmurs, kissing my forehead.

I nod, knowing I have a fuck-ton of *explaining* to do, a la *I Love Lucy* or not.

God, Colt with his ill-timed sense of humor.

It's like he has a death wish.

Hell, who am I kidding?

There's no *it's like*.

He's spent the last four years in a Russian prison.

Clearly, the man has a death wish.

Especially since he's not talking.

Royal sighs and perches on the couch arm on my other side. "You going to explain where you've been the last five years?"

"I'm trying to figure out how the fuck to start, man," Colt mutters, tearing his gaze away from me and West and shoving a hand through his hair. "Half of this shit is classified. The other half isn't exactly a pleasant memory to revisit."

My chest goes tight.

And somehow sensing that, West laces his fingers through mine, squeezing lightly.

God, he's such a good guy.

And Colt's looking at me again.

Looking at me like I've just gut punched him.

Shit.

Royal settles his hand on my shoulder and I breathe through the guilt slicing through my insides. I've done nothing wrong.

Nothing.

So why do I feel like I did?

"I think the best place to start is at the beginning," Royal says.

Banks pauses in his pacing of my living room carpet and turns to us. "So, you took the black ops job." His words are quiet. "And things clearly didn't go as planned."

Colt's gaze is on his hand for long enough that tension begins to ratchet up in the room.

Then he sighs.

"I had to go no contact during training, cut all ties to back home. But I wrote letters explaining what I could, trusted my handler to pass them on." Another sigh. "Obviously, he didn't."

"No," Royal says into the silence that falls. "He didn't."

Colt looks at him. Then at me. Then at Banks.

And the regret in his voice kills almost as much as what he shares next, some of it what I already know.

"I was supposed to infiltrate a Russian prison and extract a contact. I did the whole dumb tourist thing, breaking laws I supposedly didn't know about and getting put into that prison. Only when I got there, he was dead, and it was clear my cover was blown. In less than an hour I went from a rescue and retrieve to being a prisoner for real and..." He's staring at his hands now. "It wasn't fun."

West's hand tightens around mine and I glance at him.

He jerks his chin toward Colt, mouths, "Go to him."

The guilt in my belly is sharp and intense and it feels like it's going to slice me into a thousand pieces.

Because, God, he's *such* a good guy.

I lift our intertwined hands, press a kiss to the back of his.

Then I shore up my courage and move to Colt.

He jerks when I stop at the side of his chair, and when I sit on the arm like Royal did with me on the couch, his shoulders relax incrementally.

Going on instinct, I take his hand.

And he relaxes further, the words coming more freely.

"It was bad—sleep deprivation and beatings. They knew I had information, and they did their best to extract it. I held out as long as I could, and then I gave small shit I knew wouldn't hurt anyone, knew would buy me time. But I was running out of it, knew that if I didn't get out and do it soon, I was going to die there."

Royal curses.

Banks starts pacing again.

I just hold Colt's hand more tightly.

"Finally, a month ago, I caught a lucky break," he says quietly. "You remember Igor?"

Banks turns toward us. "The kid we played with in college?"

Colt nods. "Yeah. Turns out he's more than just a hockey player—back then *and* now."

Royal's brows fly up in surprise.

West is harder to read—his expression blank as he takes it all in.

"FSB," Colt tells us.

"I thought he was playing in the KHL?" Banks asks.

"Cover." A shrug. "Lucky for me because he heard about me, and he put his ass on the line to get me out. It was dicey. I thought it was the end for both of us more than once."

My fingers convulse around his, thinking how close we were to truly losing him.

His gaze comes to mine.

"I'm okay," he murmurs and for a moment, I have the old Colt. The one I fell in love with. The one who I could talk with until all hours of the night, discussing our dreams and ambitions, sorting our plans for the future, sharing *everything*.

Then he looks away, and the moment is broken.

"I was in bad shape when I got home—"

"No offense," Royal mutters, "but you look to be in pretty bad shape *now.*"

Colt scowls. "I'm fine."

"Right," Royal says dryly.

"You got home," Banks prompts.

A nod from Colt, though his scowl remains in place. "I got home, spent some time in the hospital, debriefed, and then searched you guys up."

"Nashville," I say softly.

Bright blue eyes come to mine. "Nashville," he says.

"But you didn't talk to Atlas."

"I didn't want to intrude. Atlas needed to focus on his woman, especially with all the press attention. I was going to follow you guys back here, but I had a setback and ended up in the hospital again."

Plain words.

But plain words that say far too much.

His hand tightens around mine. "I'm fine, baby."

My throat goes tight, and I nod.

"So, you were stalking us," Royal points out.

"I'm a spy, it's what I do." Half of Colt's mouth curves and my heart rolls over in my chest—another glimpse of the Colt of old. "Now I'm here, Banks has a fucking *kid*, Royal's marrying a country singer, Dash a movie star, and Atlas has a goddamned girlfriend."

"Believe me," Royal says. "None of us saw the girls coming."

"Maybe not," Banks agree. "Still the best shit of my life."

"Somehow I don't think the girls are going to enjoy being called *shit*," I warn him.

He flashes a smile at me. "I don't know if you know this, but Aspen kind of likes me."

Royal tosses a pillow at him. "Don't know why."

"Asshole," Banks mutters, throwing it back.

Then the conversation turns to the old days and catching up on the new ones. I slip my hand from Colt's and walk into the kitchen.

Then take a moment to finally breathe easily.

The worst is over.

Now we can move forward.

"I'm going to go."

My head jerks up and I see West standing in the doorway.

Oh, my God. West.

I forgot him again.

I'm such a shit person.

"Walk me out?" he asks softly.

And God, after all the rest of it, how can I not give him that?

It's not until we're next to his car that he says, "That's Frankie's father, isn't it?"

My mouth falls open. "How'd you—?"

"It's the eyes, sweetheart," he says gently. "Does he know?"

"Not yet," I whisper. "I know I need to tell him. I just..."

"Things have been a little nuts?" He touches the backs of his knuckles to my cheek. "Yeah, babe. I'd say they have."

"I'm sorry," I murmur, dropping my head to his chest. "I know this is a mess."

"You have nothing to apologize for."

I'm not so sure of that.

But I don't say anything, just lean against him and let him hold me tightly.

It's not until long moments later that he speaks.

And his words have the guilt slicing deeper.

"Do you want me to skip the road trip?"

"No. But thank you," I lift up, and though part of me feels awkward (or maybe it's that part of me feels wrong doing it), I brush my lips over his.

But when I drop down to my heels, I can see some of the tension has left him.

Not me though.

Because...

"I need to sort this out on my own."

TEN

COLT

Watching Briar walk West out to his car is almost more than I can stand. I think I'd rather have ten beatings than see the woman I love with someone else, but it's not her fault. He seems to care about her, treat her well, and I know damn well the guys wouldn't let her date him if he wasn't a good guy.

Too bad he's with *my* woman.

There's no universe where I don't move heaven and earth to win her back. It's just going to take some time.

"Let's get pizza," Banks says after a moment. "I don't think Briar is up to cooking."

"Yeah, pizza's a good idea." I nod, watching as he pulls out his phone, starts typing, and then puts it away without asking any of us anything.

Because he knows what everyone likes.

"Pizza will be here in fifteen," he says. "I hope you still like those disgusting little fish."

"Anchovies require a mature palate," I say primly.

He snorts. "That's probably the *only* mature part of you."

I chuckle but it's not as funny now. Me being the jokester, the guy always causing trouble, the one nobody takes seriously.

"So, uh, you want to meet Maisie?" Banks asks quietly.

Maisie.

His wife? No, that's Aspen. Maisie must be the baby.

"Well, yeah." I nod.

"Let me go get her."

While he does that, the rest of us head outside to a sprawling back patio, settling on the various chairs and couches. They obviously spend a lot of time out here, and I smile, because this suits Briar's personality well. She's a caregiver. She fell into that role as the only girl in our little family, and that much, at least, hasn't changed.

Banks is back a minute later with a squirming little bundle in his arms—and promptly hands her over to me.

When was the last time I held an infant? I can't even remember. I don't do babies. Well, I made one, I guess, but I missed her whole life. Four long years of my daughter's life. Never held her like this. Never comforted her when she cried or laughed when she giggled or—

Maisie looks up at me with eyes that are a cloudy blue color, curious but not afraid.

"Just support her head," Banks says gently, most likely noticing my hesitant movements.

I'm fascinated by her, so small and innocent, but also powerfully important to my friend. I shift, adjusting her so we're both a little more comfortable and it's amazing how sturdy she is. She's small and delicate but simultaneously hardy.

Another wave of regret.

Guilt.

Shame.

I missed all of this because I was selfish. In the moment, I thought I was being altruistic, that they would understand as soon as I was done with training and could explain. I didn't want them to try to talk me out of something so dangerous, because it felt like that was my destiny. Fighting for some theoretical cause that, in reality, means so much less than all of this.

Friends.

Family.

The incredible life they've built.

And I fucking missed all of it.

Dammit.

"Wow," I breathe finally, continuing to stare into Maisy's precious little face. "My best friend has a kid." I look up at him. "She's beautiful."

He smiles. "She is."

"And now there's another on the way." Royal's voice makes us both look up, and he smiles. Jade's on his lap and he has one hand splayed across her stomach.

"What the hell?" Banks asks, frowning. "Why didn't you tell me?"

"We were going to announce it tonight. We wanted to wait until we were all together."

"Congratulations." Banks immediately holds out his hand and Royal smacks it with his since Jade is still on his lap.

"Congratulations," I say, also extending my hand. It feels weird for Royal to smack it, our eyes meeting questioningly. Like we have to re-establish our bond. I guess that's fair.

But it still pisses me off.

"I don't think you've officially met Jade," he says after a moment. "Colt, this is Jade Cantrell, the love of my life. Honey, this is Colt Blackwood. You probably know more about him than you should."

She laughs. "It's nice to finally meet you, Colt. I'd give you a hug, but superman here has a death grip on me. He seems to think pregnancy means I'm fragile."

She has a light southern accent, bright blue eyes, and a great smile.

"I know your music," I say, smiling back. "Believe it or not,

Russian prison guards like American country music and Greek bouzouki. That's their jam."

"Russian prison guards listening to my music was *not* on my bingo card," she says.

And we all laugh.

"And this is Aspen Rockwell, soon-to-be Christianson," Banks says proudly.

"I was in no shape to plan a wedding while I was pregnant," she says, grimacing. "But it's wonderful to meet you. Banks has missed you."

There's another awkward silence and I try not to let them see me sigh. There's so much frustration inside me, practically screaming to get out, but I have to stay cool for now. I'm not strong enough to get in a boxing ring yet—one of my favorite ways to release tension—and it feels like I have to tread carefully with the guys.

And where the hell is Briar? If she's outside making out with West—

Nope. Can't go there.

She has every right to be with whomever she wants to be with.

Even if it kills me to watch it.

"Before we eat." Jade nudges Royal and he lets her up. She reaches into a bag I hadn't noticed before, pulling out some kind of clothing. "We have T-shirts!"

"Let me see!" Aspen snatches one and then bursts out laughing. "Aw, I can't wait to wear mine!" She holds it up against her chest and it says 'World's Best Auntie.' The guys' shirts say 'World's Best Uncle' and they are pink and blue, respectively.

There isn't one for me, of course, and I think Jade realizes that around the same time I do because her eyes meet mine apologetically.

"We'll order one more," she says softly.

I nod, because what else can I do?

"Pizza's here," Briar says, coming inside carrying three large boxes. "And one of them says 'anchovies' on the outside." She gives me a disgusted look. "Seriously? Four years in prison didn't cure you of this horrible habit?"

I blink for a moment, unsure if she's serious but before I can respond everyone cracks up.

"Don't blame me if your palate is less sophisticated than mine." I shrug.

Banks gets up and takes the pizzas from her so she can set out plates and napkins for us.

"Frankie!" Briar yells into the house. "Time to eat."

A minute later Frankie skips onto the patio and my heart squeezes. I'm still holding Maisie, who seems pretty content in my arms, and I can only imagine what it would have been like to hold Frankie at this age.

Did Briar think of me as she held her newborn daughter? Wishing I was there? Or was she angry at the way I left her? I still have so many questions and not nearly enough time to ask them.

"What are *those*?" Frankie asks, wrinkling her nose when Banks opens the box containing half of the pizza with everything.

"That's called an anchovy," I say. "You should try it. It's really yummy."

She screws up her face in disgust but leans forward to inspect it more carefully. "Is it...a fish?"

"A type of fish, yes. Hasn't your mother introduced you to anchovies?"

"One bite to be polite," Frankie murmurs, as if that's something she's said often.

"Go ahead, sweetie," I say softly. "They're good. A little salty. No bones or anything."

Everyone freezes, watching in fascination as Frankie picks one of the anchovies off the pizza. Then she pops it into her mouth and begins to chew.

Briar's eyes are wide, staring as if she can't quite believe what she's seeing. Everyone else has similar expressions, but mostly, I'm focused on my daughter. No one's confirmed anything, but it's pretty obvious. I'm just waiting for the right moment to ask Briar.

Frankie chews slowly, thoughtfully, and then swallows and cocks her head. "Very salty," she says. "But not bad. Can I have a piece?"

"Sure." I grin, turning to stick my tongue out at Briar.

"Mommy, can I have some juice with this? It's yummy." Frankie seems oblivious.

That's my girl. Now there's definitely no doubt she's mine.

"Uh, sure." Briar and Aspen hurry inside and I can hear them trying to disguise their laughter the minute they're around the corner.

"Let me take the baby so you can eat," Banks says, starting to get up.

"Nah, I'm good. She's warm and cuddly and smells good. I like holding her." I grab a piece of pizza with one hand and take a big bite, watching my daughter happily eating anchovy pizza.

My daughter.

Not being able to talk to Briar about this is driving me crazy, but since no one has said a word, some sixth sense tells me to tread carefully. Maybe they think Frankie doesn't know? She most certainly guessed, if that's the case. But Briar and I haven't had a moment to confirm or deny it.

In spite of me living in her house, we haven't had time to talk about many of the things I want to bring up.

"Colt?" Frankie looks up at me with guileless blue eyes.

"Yeah, honey?"

"Do you play Connect Four?"

Banks chokes on his pizza, chuckling.

I give him a strange look but then look down at Frankie. "It's been a really long time, but sure. I played it a lot when I was a kid."

"Good." She gives me a smile I can't quite decipher, kind of like Cinderella meets Lucifer—it would be disconcerting if it were anyone else. "We can play after dinner."

"Okay?" I look at Banks, but he just laughs.

"Go with it," Royal murmurs, clapping me on the shoulder before grabbing some pizza.

Pizza and Connect Four.

Not the way I pictured my return to the family, but it's pretty cool, nonetheless. If I could just get Dash and Atlas to forgive me, everything would be great.

But something tells me that's going to be a lot harder than anything else.

Eleven

BRIAR

I'm doing the dishes.

All six of the cups and the fork that Frankie used to scoop up some of the leftover anchovy guts—barf—after she ate two slices of pizza.

God, of course I have a kid who likes anchovies.

Blech.

But that's not what has me furiously scrubbing the tines of the fork, trying to erase each and every bit of that anchovy gunk.

It's that I just sat around on my back patio, eating pizza, laughing with the girls and Frankie, the boys and *Colt* during Sunday Dinner.

Freaking Sunday Dinner.

Something I created because I wanted Frankie to have what Dash and I didn't—a family that comes together on the regular.

It's not every Sunday.

But it's a lot of them.

And I felt like it was critically important, especially because she didn't have a dad.

But now—

A throat clears and I whip around to see Colt leaning against the wall.

"You should be in bed," I murmur.

He looks exhausted, and just the day before, he was bleeding in the sheets of his motel room.

Now, he's been out of bed all afternoon and evening, the explosive surprise of his return from the dead transforming into hanging out with the guys and getting caught up on some of what he missed. There's too much for him to be really up to speed, and he may never get there, considering all he's missed, but he got some highlights tonight.

And then Frankie roped him into Connect Four.

He let her win precisely once—because most of her victims (yes, *victims*) learn that she's a shark within that first match. And then he, even though he brought out the big guns, he still lost to her four more times, taking her out only once.

But even though he got destroyed in a board game by a four-year-old, he seemed unbothered.

No, he seemed like he was having the time of his life.

Like he was soaking up every moment.

And...more guilt.

"I'm not tired yet," he says.

I turn back to the sink, to washing that fork, scrubbing like a maniac. "You were barely able to walk yesterday. You need to rest."

"I think the whole sleeping like the dead for eighteen hours topped me up, baby."

My heart lurches at his soft *baby* but I don't stop cleaning.

Or pretending to because the fork is *sparkling*.

"Baby," I hear.

But this time it's not from across the room.

It's from right next to me.

Millimeters from my ear.

And he's stepping close, his chest against my back, hands resting on my shoulders for a moment before they slide down the outsides of my arms, covering my hands...and wrestling the fork from my grip.

"You got it, Thorny," he murmurs once it's free and on the drying rack. Then he's reaching forward, turning off the water.

Which means I'm surrounded by him.

Held close to him.

God, it's been so long.

And I've missed him so much.

And—

He shifts, pushing off me and turning so that he's leaning back against the edge of the counter.

Still close.

Just...not holding me.

And am I a shit person if I say that I miss it?

He clears his throat again, and I realize that I'm staring. Thank God Banks and Royal took their women home.

Thank *God* that Frankie demanded her Uncle Royal do his bedtime routine so that my little girl is asleep.

Thank God—

"Briar," he says, and his tone is filled with warning.

"What?" I ask, the warmth I was feeling at being held close to him fading. Annoyance taking its place.

His brows flick up, clearly feeling that annoyance...and lobbing some of his own back in my direction when he asks, "Something you want to tell me?"

My throat goes tight.

Because I know *exactly* what he's talking about.

Exactly what he must have picked up on.

Frankie's hair.

Frankie's eyes.

Frankie's penchant for freaking anchovies.

So, I don't make him work for it.

"I didn't know I was pregnant until I was almost thirteen weeks along," I whisper and watch as his entire body goes rigid. "I...there was never any doubt that I'd keep it, keep *her*." My eyes close and I remember that appointment with my obstetrician, seeing the black and white image on the ultrasound machine.

The tiny baby.

That fluttering heartbeat.

"We made her," I say, looking up into his deep blue eyes. "She came from a night that meant so much to me, from a man who meant the world to me, so no, there was never any doubt I would have her."

"Meant?" he asks, and I shut my eyes, clenching them tightly together, wishing that things were different.

That so many things were different.

"Colt," I whisper, and he must hear the pain in my voice because he's quiet for a long moment.

Then he asks, "What happened then?"

"I tried to get in touch with you," I tell him. "I left a message. I left *messages.*"

He touches my cheek and my lids peel back, the regret on his face heavy. "I'm sorry, baby."

I nod, acknowledging that, but having to get the rest of this out. "I didn't hear anything—not for months—and th-then...you were dead."

He sighs then takes my hand, kissing the back of it.

Another apology in his eyes, but he doesn't say it out loud. Instead, he asks, "Do the guys know? Is that why Dash and Atlas want to kill me?"

"No," I say. "They don't know. I never told anyone who Frankie's dad was."

"They let you get away with that?"

"I don't know if you remember"—my words are light—"but I can be a bit stubborn."

"A bit?" he teases, and I gently swat at him.

Then sigh.

And give him the rest of it.

"After a while everyone stopped asking," I say. "So no, my

brother and Atlas, how pissed they both are at you...that's all on you."

He chuckles. "Unfortunately, I was worried that might be the case." Then his expression gentles, and he touches my cheek again. "You did a great job with her, Thorny. She's amazing."

My lungs hitch, and my heart squeezes and...

God, he's missed so much.

And I've missed him.

And I've wished that he was here to meet Frankie too many times to count.

"She's funny and whip smart and beautiful and I'm so sorry that you had to do it all alone—"

"I wasn't alone," I whisper.

He stills, and I want to take the words back when pain ripples across his face, but before I can, he tucks a strand of my hair behind my ear. "The family you've built is beautiful, baby, but I'm still so fucking sorry you've borne the truth alone for all these years."

"I'm not," I tell him. "That was our night, and it meant everything. I didn't want to share it with anyone."

His eyes blaze into mine.

Then he cups my jaw and leans close, his words brushing over my lips. "That night meant everything to me too."

That's all I've ever wanted to hear.

All I've ever needed.

But when he bends to close the distance between our mouths, I put my hand up to stop him.

I want nothing more than to taste him again.

But I can't.

Not right now.

Not when—

"I'm with West now."

TWELVE

COLT

Despite how exhausted I am, sleep is a long time coming. I toss, turn, and doze, getting up to go to the bathroom like I've suddenly got the bladder of a ninety-year-old. My dreams are riddled with a kaleidoscope of images: the prison, Igor showing up to rescue me, the night Briar and I spent together, Briar kissing West.

It's frustrating, and the physical pain isn't doing anything to help my state of mind.

I'm with West now.

Those words play over and over in my head, until I want to punch something. Mostly West. But this isn't his fault.

I'm with West now.

So close to kissing her, touching her, having her in my arms—her words hit me like a slap in the face.

Regret slices through me.

If you break it down to the very basics, I chose a job over the woman I love. My friends. In my defense, I truly thought I could have it all. I'd have to keep some secrets, but it's no different than being in the military. That's what I told myself.

Now I know better.

And it's too late.

I'm with West now.

At some point, I must have fallen asleep, and when I wake up, I hear that same breathing next to my bed that I heard yesterday morning.

Frankie.

I smile to myself before turning over and prying my lids open.

"You didn't answer my question."

"Good morning to you too." I smile at the grumpy look on her face.

"Well?"

"What question, kiddo?"

"Are you my daddy?"

There's no way I'm having a conversation like this without Briar, and that means getting my ass in gear.

"I'm going to need you to turn around," I say.

"How come?"

"Because I need to put pants on."

"This again?" she huffs. "Why do you never wear pants?"

Out of the mouths of babes...

"You and I are going to have to set some boundaries," I murmur.

"Frankie!" Briar comes in, hands on her hips. "What have I told you about opening closed doors?"

"But this is our house!" Frankie protests. "And you said he's your friend."

"It is and he is—but he still gets to have some privacy when he's sleeping."

"Fine." Frankie huffs more dramatically this time, flouncing out of the room.

Briar and I exchange a look and then chuckle.

"Sorry about that," she says. "She's really curious about you. But I'll leave you to rest."

"No, I'm up," I say quickly. "I just need a few minutes to get dressed."

"All right. See you when you're ready." She leaves the room, gently closing the door behind her.

After our almost-kiss last night, we both made excuses, going to our separate bedrooms, but she seems normal this morning, no hint of annoyance in her demeanor.

I make short work of washing up and pulling on clean clothes. Then I pad out to the kitchen, where Frankie and Briar are side-by-side at the counter. I'm not sure what they're making, but there's batter involved and Frankie is giggling. They're kind of adorable in matching pink and white ruffled aprons, Frankie standing on a stool that's the perfect height for her to help.

Watching them, I feel the strangest blend of sadness and joy. This was supposed to be my life, and I walked away to be some kind of hero. What the hell was I thinking?

Some kind of caramel mixture gets on Frankie's nose and Briar playfully wipes it away, licking it off her fingers. They laugh together, and in that moment—faces close together, hair in similar ponytails—there is no doubt they're mother and daughter. Frankie looks like me, but she has her mother's smile and mannerisms.

"Good morning again." Briar turns with a smile. "I hope you like French toast."

"Love it," I say, walking over to inspect what they're doing. "Although, I can't remember the last time I had it."

"Well, this is stuffed with a cream cheese mixture and topped with my special caramel-cream."

My mouth waters.

"Sounds like heaven."

"It's my favorite!" Frankie announces.

"Her *current* favorite," Briar corrects, laughing.

"It used to be blueberry pancakes but that's when I was little. I'm big now." She dips her finger in the caramel mixture and holds it out to me.

Yup, this child is going to wrap me around her finger in no time.

I lick her fingers and moan dramatically. "Holy fu—er, crap, that's good. I'm going to get fat if I stay here much longer."

"You have to exercise," Frankie says, nodding. "Uncle Banks makes all the uncles work out. Mommy doesn't like getting sweaty, though."

Briar gives her the side eye. "Hey, you're not supposed to tell all my secrets!"

A timer goes off, and Briar pulls a pan out of the oven.

My stomach growls.

When was the last time someone cooked for me?

Never? Certainly not my mother. Dash's parents invited me over a handful of times, but those were big events, not something specifically for me. And none of us cooked in college.

A sudden wave of emotion I can't identify fills my chest and I turn away. I'm not big on feelings—but Briar is the exception to that. Hell, she's the exception to every rule, every decision, everything I thought I knew about myself.

"You can make yourself a cup of coffee," she calls over her shoulder to me, "while the French toast cools a little. And Frankie will set the table."

"Okay." Frankie jumps down and reaches for dishes that were already out.

She meticulously sets three place settings—a dish, napkin, fork, and butter knife—and then climbs up on a stool.

I make coffee, Briar serves up the French toast, and then the three of us gather round one side of the island.

The three of us.

My kid and the woman I love.

This was supposed to be my life, and I just walked away. Almost died before I could tell her how I felt.

I won't make that mistake again.

"So. Is anyone going to answer my question?" Frankie asks after inhaling the first piece of French toast.

"What question?" Briar asks in confusion.

I cough lightly, because I know what's coming even if she doesn't.

"Is. He. My. Daddy?"

Briar and I exchange a look, and I give her a barely perceptible nod. It's time. Frankie already knows. And there's no use hiding it anymore because regardless of what happens with Briar and me, I'm not going anywhere. I'm going to be as much a part of Frankie's life as Briar allows.

"He is," Briar says after a long moment.

"I knew it." Frankie's lips tighten and she puts her fork down with a little thud. "So where *were* you? Did you not want to be my daddy?"

Oh, hell.

I'd definitely rather get another prison beating than let her think I didn't want to be her father. It's all I've thought about since yesterday morning.

"No, sweetie. That's not it at all. Not even close."

"Then why?" The look she gives me reminds me of Briar when she's really upset. Cheeks a little flushed, eyes wide, lips pressed together tightly.

It would be adorable if it didn't break my heart into a million pieces.

"It was work," I say slowly, scrambling to figure out how to explain being a spy to a four-year-old. "I have a very special kind of job and—"

"*Work?* For four and three-quarter years?"

Technically, more than that, but I'm not going to point that out.

"Sweetie, it's complicated," I begin.

"Grown-ups always say that when they don't want to tell me the truth," she says, staring me down. "And Mommy always says that work is *never* more important than family. Never ever. So, I don't believe you."

With that, she climbs down off the stool and walks out of the kitchen.

"Briar, what do we do?" I ask quietly.

"Let her cool off. She has my temper," she admits, resting her elbows on the counter. "Normally, I wouldn't let her get away with being rude to a guest or getting up in the middle of breakfast, but I think she gets a pass today. This is a lot for her to take in. She's incredibly bright, and very mature for her age, but this turns her life upside down."

"Has she...asked about me? I mean, in general?"

Briar nods. "Not a lot, but once she started Pre-K this year, and she saw all the other daddies, she asked me about hers."

"What did you tell her?"

"That he loved her very much, but he died."

That explains how she knew.

Neither of us say anything for a while.

"Should I go after her?" I ask finally.

"I don't know if she's ready for that. She's processing a lot of emotions."

"What should I do?"

"The thing with kids is consistency. Showing up. Letting her know you're not going to leave her. They have to feel safe, wanted, and secure. And security is something that takes time. You're going to have to earn her trust."

The way she looks at me when she says the last part is telling —she's letting me know that I'm going to have to earn *her* trust too.

"I'm not going anywhere," I promise, reaching out to lay one of my hands on hers. "I swear it, Briar. I'm back for good, done with the spy game. I can't explain that part to her, though."

"No." Briar is thoughtful. "When the time is right, and she's a little more open to listening, we'll talk about the marines. She knows Uncle Dash is super proud to have been a marine, and we can give her a watered down version of being in prison."

"Okay. You'll have to guide me, Briar. I've been a dad for a day and I'm a little lost."

"Well, the first thing you're going to have to learn is that you can't sleep naked." Her eyes twinkle with mirth and I chuckle.

"Normally, I don't do that when I'm a guest at someone's home. It's just been tough to bend and twist in the middle of the night. I'll make the effort, though."

"Good." She puts the last bite of breakfast in her mouth, wipes her lips, and then pushes her plate away. "I'm going to go talk to her."

"You don't want me to come?"

She hesitates. "No. I think I need to take this one. Maybe we can try again at dinner."

"All right."

I watch her go thoughtfully.

The one part of this that I'm holding on to is that she hasn't said a word about me finding somewhere else to stay, and she didn't seem at all upset about my intention to be part of Frankie's life.

If only I knew what she was thinking—about me and about the future.

Thirteen

Briar

My talk with Frankie doesn't go well.

My little girl is sad and hopeful and scared and mad...and I'm right there with her. My emotions are at an all-time high, and then add in the lovely guilt I'm carrying around about West and—

Fun. Fun.

Anyway, I debated keeping Frankie home from school today, both of us playing hooky and basically keeping her captive until she let go of her stubbornness and talked to me.

But I wasn't joking with Colt earlier.

She gets that recalcitrant streak from me.

And battering against it doesn't work.

Heaven help me when she's a teenager. I'm going to have my hands full as a single—

I still, my hands clutched tight on the steering wheel, and drop my forehead to the leather circle.

Thank God, I was late dropping Frankie off and my car is the only one in the preschool's lot.

No one to see me have my existential crisis.

Because I'm not a single mom any longer.

Because Colt is back.

Because Frankie knows the truth of him being her dad and that secret I carried for nearly five years is coming out.

I groan, eyes stinging.

I want to sit here, to sit in my misery, to keep beating myself up.

If I'd told them earlier then I wouldn't be worrying about protecting Colt from my four brothers wanting to murder him for daring to touch their little sister, for daring to do a *lot* more than just touch.

They are going to *flip* out.

I know it's going to be like the scene in my kitchen, that it might even be worse than that.

And I know I'm out of time, that the truth is out of my control, that me wanting to think and think and *think* about the best way to approach this, about all the possible outcomes, both negative and positive, isn't going to be possible.

I need action.

I need words.

I need a goddamned plan.

And I need it fast.

So, I only have one choice.

I need to call a meeting of the Gamebreaker Girls—maybe someday I won't be in a panic and will be able to come up with something cute and pithy that can rival the guys and their Game-breakers monikers, but I'm functioning on too little sleep and too many emotions and the existential dread that my brothers are going to kill the man I love—

Loved.

"Fuck," I whisper, guilt surging to the top of those swirling emotions.

Because I need to talk to West.

I *need* to sort out my head.

And my heart.

God, do I ever.

So, I do the only thing I can—I stay in that parking lot but lift my head from the steering wheel so I can send a text...and then a bunch more.

And the next thing I know, I'm driving to Banks and Aspen's house.

And the girls are all going to meet me there.

———

Thirty minutes later, I'm holding Maisie in my arms, not above soothing myself with the adorable nugget that's my niece.

Especially since four women I love and respect are staring at me.

Waiting for me to spill my guts.

And I don't know where to start.

Maisie burrows into the crook of my elbow and my eyes start to burn.

Frankie used to be this little.

And Colt missed it—missed all of it.

"Briar, honey," Willow says gently, breaking the silence. "You wanted to talk?"

I nod, smoothing my fingers through the peach fuzz on the top of Maisie's head. "I do," I agree softly. "I *need* to. I just...I don't know where to start."

"Does it have to do with Colt?" Aspen asks, her tone pitched toward careful.

Extremely careful.

As though, one wrong word is going to set me off.

I frown, start to open my mouth, but Lily beats me to the punch.

"You think?" she says dryly.

"He did reappear from the dead," Jade says, clearly lightening the mood.

But Lily—as usual—is not to be swayed. "Do you all not have *eyes?* Of course, this has to do with Colt."

A furrow appears between Jade's brows. "What do you mean?"

"The eyes, the hair, those lashes." She pushes up out of the armchair she occupied and comes over, stealing Maisie from my arms, the stink, and she doesn't miss a beat when she does on, "The *anchovies* on the freaking pizza?"

Jade's eyes go wide.

Willow nibbles at the corner of her mouth. "Are you saying—?"

"That our little Thorny and big, bad Colt did the nasty and that nasty resulted in our adorable but extremely beautiful and smart, like her mama, and fierce and brave, clearly like her *daddy?*" She pauses, gently swaying back and forth in that instinctively motherly way that many women seem to adopt around babies—and God, when she and Atlas get around to having kids, she's going to be a natural. "Yeah, sweetie, that's *exactly* what I'm saying."

Willow's eyes are wide, and they drift to mine.

Jade looks surprised but also not as surprised as I would have thought—like somewhere in the back of her mind, she expected this.

Aspen...well, I can't get a read on her.

At least until she says, "Well, one good thing is that Banks and I already kind of knew, months ago, but we figured that was your business to share so we didn't say anything or push."

"What?" we all say in unison.

"Briar, honey," she says, gently tugging Maisie out of Lily's arms and cuddling her baby close. "We knew you had your reasons for not sharing, and while Banks wasn't thrilled when we put the pieces together, he also understood. He always said you two had something special."

"And you held out on sharing *that* piece of juicy gossip with the rest of us?" Lily accuses.

"Lily," Willow begins.

"Seriously!" Jade chimes in. "I agree with Lily! This is something we should have known."

"No," Aspens says firmly. "We shouldn't have. It was Briar's business and right now she's asking for our help."

Lily scowls.

And Jade is right there with her.

Willow seems halfway between concern and scowl, something that would have normally amused me.

If I wasn't worried about my brothers murdering the father of my child.

"Right," Aspen says, sinking down onto the couch but letting Jade commandeer Maisie. "The first thing I'll do is let Banks know that we all know, so that's one less that you have to worry about."

"Frankie's upset," I whisper. "And Dash and Atlas couldn't even look at him."

Lily sighs. "You know Atlas will come around, sweetheart."

"I hope so."

"And Frankie's bound to be upset," Jade says. "But she also has her mama's big heart, so we know it won't be long before she comes around. Give her time, maybe talk to a therapist—I'm sure Royal's can give us a recommendation as a starting point. And we'll all be patient and encouraging without putting too much pressure on her."

I nod because I know she's right.

It's just...

"What if they hate me?" I blurt. "I mean, *me* having been with Colt."

"What does *that* mean?" Willow asks, her tone far fiercer than I've ever heard it.

"I was a nerd in high school, glasses and frumpy clothes and thirty extra pounds. I didn't have a boyfriend, didn't go on a date until college. I didn't even kiss anyone—not until I got laser eye surgery and tamed my hair and lost the baby fat. Not because I didn't want to, but because no one gave me the time of day to have that."

"Honey," Willow says, taking my hand.

"And Colt," I whisper. "He was their beautiful, gorgeous friend and he treated me the same before and after I made the transformation from ugly duckling to a woman finally comfortable in my own skin. We always joked and bantered and talked about everything and nothing and all the stuff in between. He always saw *me*"—I thump a hand against my chest—"and then finally, *finally* for two days and one night, I had him, had the fantasy of him, of us, had the plans we made for a future together. And then...I lost him."

Willow's eyes are glassy. "You lost someone you loved, but you also lost your dream."

I nod.

"They won't hate that you had that, sweetheart," Jade says. "Because that's the most beautiful and saddest thing I've ever heard."

Willow brushes a tear away and nods in agreement.

"I think we could write a few platinum songs and an Oscar-winning film to boot with all of that angst," Lily says dryly.

"Lily!" Jade snaps.

She shrugs. "You know I'm not wrong—hell, you're already probably writing the lyrics in your head as we speak."

The slight flush on Jade's cheeks tells me that, indeed, Lily isn't wrong.

"It's okay, you guys," I say, bravely soldiering on. Because I've had too many years of doing just that to stop now.

And anyway, the truth is out.

They know where my head was back then—and is now.

"But we still need to find a way to tell the rest of the guys without it ending in a brawl. Colt is still recovering, and he doesn't need to land back in the hospital."

"Unfortunately," Lily says. "I do think that Atlas is angry enough to throw a punch." A beat. "Or ten."

"I've never seen Hudson as mad as he was last night," Willow groans.

"Royal took the news okay," Jade says. "But he's so protective of you and Frankie. Hearing that Colt..." She trails off and nibbles at the corner of her mouth.

"It's going to be fine," Aspen says.

And I'm not the only one whose mouth drops open as our gazes go to hers.

"I have a plan," she tells us. "We have a new bourbon rep coming to the Sapphire Room. Banks and I will tell the guys they need to come in for a tasting since I can't while I'm breast-feeding—"

"Didn't you just get drunk off your ass like a few days ago?" Lily asks.

Aspen smirks. "All I have to do is mention my breasts and some female bodily function and Royal and Dash will forget all about that."

"And Atlas?" Jade asks, and for the record, she doesn't argue Aspen's point.

I don't either.

Because my brother may be tough, but female stuff scares the shit out of him.

"You think I'll ask Atlas for help and he'll turn me down?" she says. "Especially with Banks out of town with the Vipers?"

Lily glances over at me. "Oh, she's good."

I nod.

Because Lily's right.

The only problem...

Now I'll have to tell my brothers the truth.

FOURTEEN

COLT

I come awake slowly. Suspiciously.

No soft, harried breathing.

No big blue eyes waiting inches from my face.

The guest room is empty and that hurts more than all my other aches and pains put together.

It's quiet this morning, though, making me wonder if the girls are already gone, back to their normal routine.

That's depressing.

They have a routine, and I don't even know what it is. Frankie goes to school, and Briar works for—*with*, she works with—Atlas, but she doesn't seem to have strict hours.

If I'm going to insert myself into their lives, I have to learn the ins and outs of the life they lead. Quickly. It would be great to lounge around for a week or two, getting my strength back and starting to look for a place to live, but I don't have that luxury.

Money isn't an issue. I have plenty. A lot. In fact, more than I've ever seen in my life. Certainly not the many millions Banks makes or the billions Atlas has amassed, but for a kid from Ohio who literally grew up using hand-me-down hockey sticks, I made a lot of money while I was letting the FSB beat and torture me. My handlers even took the opportunity to invest it for me, so the two million in my account almost mocks me.

Almost.

I'm not stupid, though. That kind of money won't last a lifetime. I still have to figure out my next steps. I'd assumed—probably stupidly—that Dash or Atlas would be able to help me find something. Now I'm not so sure. Hell, I'm not sure of anything at this point.

I drag my sorry ass out of bed and into the shower. That helps loosen up the stiffness, so I feel halfway human.

Lights are on in the kitchen, and I walk in to find Frankie by herself, coloring.

"Good morning, honey," I say cautiously.

She doesn't look up. "Good morning."

At least she has manners, even if she's still pissed.

"Whatcha coloring?" I stare down at the stick figures on the page.

"My family."

"Show me who everyone is," I say carefully.

"Mommy and me." She points. "Uncle Banks." He has on a crude but effective hockey jersey with his number on it. "Auntie Aspen and baby Maisie." Aspen still has her pregnancy belly even though she's holding the baby. "Uncle Royal and Auntie Jade with their baby." She made a big circle for Jade's belly, drawing a stick figure baby inside. "Uncle Atlas and Lily." Atlas is the only one other than banks that's wearing clothes—and it's a rudimentary suit. "Uncle Dash and Auntie Willow." Well, I guess that's a lie—Willow has on red high heels. "And Fruit Loop."

"Fruit Loop?"

She finally looks up, eyeing me like I'm stupid. "My goldfish. My other one died but Uncle Royal got me another one." She points, and sure enough, there's a goldfish in a bowl on the counter.

"My family." She shrugs and goes back to coloring, though she pushes the now finished family portrait to the side.

Ouch.

I guess Daddy didn't make the cut.

What did you expect? The devil on my shoulder asks smugly. *You left them.*

Well, nothing to be done about that now.

"Where's Mommy?" I ask.

"Blow drying her hair. That takes a *long* time."

"Have you had breakfast?"

"No."

"Are you hungry?"

"Do you even know how to cook?"

"I make a pretty mean waffle."

"The frozen kind?"

This kid really is a ball-buster, but that's okay. I kind of like that in a woman.

"Not the frozen kind, smarty-pants," I say, ruffling her hair. "I make them from scratch. Want to help me?"

"Nope." She's not looking up again, but that's okay.

Consistency, Briar said. Letting her know I'm not going anywhere, even when she's having a tantrum. Or being difficult. I'm sure this won't be the last time.

I make a cup of coffee and start scouring Briar's cupboards for the ingredients I need. It's funny—this is one of the only things I remember from my childhood. Before my dad died and everything went to hell. Before grief sent my mom off the deep end of alcoholism. Before the beatings and—

No. I'm not going to re-live that. She had her demons, I have mine. I'm not bringing that into my relationship with my daughter.

Luckily, Briar has a very well-stocked pantry. Now if I can just find the mixer.

"Frankie, do you know where Mommy keeps the mixer?"

Still not looking up, she uses one hand to point.

I don't know whether to laugh or cry, but I get out the mixer and then go back into the pantry. I saw some white chocolate chips. I don't usually add them, but this might be fun. Especially since I know there are strawberries in the fridge.

The waffle iron is on the counter, so I heat it while I mix everything together. Then, as the first batch is cooking, I get another bowl to make fresh whipped cream—with a touch of melted white chocolate. Briar loves fresh whipped cream, and white chocolate is her favorite.

Well, it was.

People don't just change their love for chocolate, do they?

Hopefully not.

"What are you doing?" Frankie demands, and I realize she's standing next to me.

"Making fresh whipped cream."

"I don't like whipped cream."

"That's okay—your mom does."

"How do you know?"

"Because your mom and I have been friends for a long time. Since long before you were born. I know lots of things about her."

"What's her favorite color?"

"Green."

Frankie seems surprised I know the answer.

"What does she put on her hot dogs?"

"Chili and cheddar cheese."

She makes a noise that sounds a little like "hmph," as if it flusters her that I have the answers to her questions.

"Can I do the next one?" she asks as I put the first batch of waffles on a plate.

"Sure." I help her lift the bowl, and she carefully pours some batter into the iron. We close it together, since I don't want her to get burned, and then stand there watching it. Maybe it's going to do a trick.

"What do you want on your waffle?" I ask while we wait.

"Butter and syrup."

"Coming right up." The syrup is already out, and I grab some butter from the fridge. "You want me to fix it for you or do you do it yourself?"

Her brows knit together. "Mommy always does it for me."

"Mommy's drying her hair. I'm happy to do it or let you do it. What do you prefer?" I'm treating her like she's a lot older than four, but she acts a lot older than four.

"I guess you can do it." She climbs back up on her stool while I fix her plate.

"One waffle or two?"

"Two, please."

"Do I need to cut them up for you?"

"No, thank you." She lifts the knife, but I can see she's struggling. I also note that she's left-handed.

Like me.

"You're a lefty," I say casually. "That makes things a little harder."

She nods solemnly. "You have no idea."

I chuckle. "Actually, I do. I'm left-handed too. Here, let me show you." I lean over her from behind, taking both her hands in mine, demonstrating what I consider to be the best way to hold the knife and fork.

"Oh! That's easier!" she says, excitement in her voice.

"Great." I turn to grab the next batch of waffles just as Briar comes in.

"Good morning," she says cautiously, looking from me to Frankie and back again.

"You still love white chocolate?" I ask her.

"Is that even a question?" she asks, laughing as she makes herself a cup of coffee.

"Just checking. I made white chocolate whipped cream to go with the waffles. And I cut up some strawberries."

Her eyes widen as she looks around. "This is...lovely. Thank you."

"Your hair looks really pretty," I say, winking.

Her cheeks turn pink. "Th-thank you."

Compliments still make her stutter.

Have the men in her life in the last five years not showered her with compliments? Made her feel beautiful? Let her know how desirable she is?

While I hate the thought of another man touching her, I hate the thought of anyone not treating her like the goddess she is even more. Weren't the boys looking out for her?

We settle at the end of the island again, just like yesterday, and dig in.

"These are so good," Briar moans. "I'd forgotten about your dad's waffle recipe."

I grin. "Right?"

"You have a daddy?" Frankie asks.

"Of course. Everyone has a daddy. But mine died when I was nine."

"You died when I was zero," she says flatly.

"I was a prisoner of war," I correct gently. "I don't know if you understand what that means."

She shakes her head, but her eyes are on mine, curious. Interested. Trying to understand.

And that's a great start.

"It means that there was an enemy when I was in the marines, and during a fight, they caught me. They kept me prisoner for four years and wouldn't let me write letters or call home."

Her eyes are wide and filled with confusion.

God, I hate that. But what else can I say? She's four. I think using words like spy or black ops or military intelligence would just confuse her.

"That's mean," she finally whispers.

"It is. But then a friend came and rescued me—and now I'm back."

There's a long, awkward silence as she studies my face, as if searching for answers to all the questions she has.

"Are you going to leave again?"

I flick a quick glance in Briar's direction and note she's stopped eating, watching me carefully.

I don't think I've ever been more afraid to answer a question in my life.

But I can't let my girls down.

Not now, not ever again.

I won't.

"I guess that depends on if you guys want me to stick around."

Fifteen

Briar

I suck in a breath and try to calm myself as I walk into the Sapphire Room.

Funny story, it doesn't work.

Mostly because I'm shitting myself.

I dropped Frankie at Aspen's place after work, stopped by the house to change and tell Colt I had something to do.

And now I'm here.

Doing it.

Of course, we had an argument before I left, him rightly guessing that I was going to tell the boys he was the father and pissed that I was trying to do it without him.

I shouldn't have gone home to change after work.

I just...well, part of me wanted out of my heels.

The rest—

The rest needed to see him.

And that urge—and wrestling with the guilt of it and what it means for West and me along with the effort it took to convince him that I needed to do this alone—means I'm running late.

And I *hate* running late.

Hate that I have to have this conversation.

Hate—

A lot.

And none of that is going to do anything but make me more stressed out, more *late*.

"Enough," I whisper and force myself to turn the corner and walk into the club. It's quiet because the crowd doesn't really pick up until after dinner time, and I can't decide if that's good or bad.

Good because there will be less people to witness my brothers freaking out, planning a murder...and then potentially going out to conduct said murder.

Bad because I won't have too many people to intervene if the talk of murder turns my way.

They won't leave Frankie an orphan, right?

"Briar!"

Shaking myself at Dash's impatient voice, I hurry over to our table. The table that none of the guys are actually sitting down at.

Probably because it has a bronze plaque that says *Reserved for Colt* affixed to its top.

Yikes.

"What's up?" I ask my brother when I'm within speaking (instead of bellowing distance).

"Aspen's no-showed," he says with a scowl. "And the fucking bourbon rep no-showed too."

Right.

Our subterfuge.

I didn't really think about what would happen after the meeting that drew them all here, didn't actually happen.

Or that—given the annoyed expressions on the three men's faces—how that would impact the starting tone of our conversation.

"Do you know where she is?" Atlas asks, still in a suit, and clearly not having going home to change.

Yikes again.

Apparently, Lily didn't give him a mind-blowing orgasm to soften the edges of his grumpy.

"Um, yes," I admit, earning three annoyed expressions again.

Though at least Royal's is edging away from irritated.

Instead, his blue eyes are shrouded, as though he's preparing for something.

Well, the man *better*.

Because I'm about to tell them something that will make them incredibly unhappy.

Or...maybe not?

Maybe, like Banks, they already know, and just didn't want to say anything?

Maybe—

"Well?" Dash demands.

"Well, what?" I ask.

"Well," Atlas says, waving an impatient hand, "where the fuck is she?"

Watching my daughter so I can tell you guys I banged your best friend and got knocked up, and funny story, that's why we're all here tonight, folks!

Which is a thought I'm keeping in my head.

Deep in my head.

"Thorny," Royal says and though it's calm, there's a note of impatience there. "Talk to us."

"Right," I whisper. Then exhale and focus. "I need to tell you guys something."

And great...more tension.

It swirls through the air like an almost palpable force, clenching at my throat, my stomach, clawing its way through my insides.

"Can we all sit down?" I say.

Atlas crosses his arms but, for the record, doesn't move, just glares at me.

Dash adopts a similar expression, though he does it with his hands on his hips.

Royal studies me for a long moment—eyes unreadable—then sighs quietly and sinks down into the chair he always sits at when we come to the Sapphire Room.

"Guys," he says when Atlas and Dash don't move (probably because they don't want anything to do with Colt), and though they go into a long standoff with glares exchanged all around, eventually they move to the table and sit down.

I don't miss that Atlas sets the black leather cocktail menu sitting at its center on its side.

Covering the plaque with Colt's name on it.

Oh, this is so not going to go well.

But I need to do it.

And the best way to deal with tough shit is to put my head down and just...get down to it.

So, I shore my spine, take another fortifying breath, and get down to it.

"I should have told you guys this a long time ago," I say quietly, glancing at each of them in turn before I direct my gaze down to my hands, searching for the right words, trying to choose them carefully. "I...at first I didn't know why I so stubbornly kept the truth close to my chest, except that it felt like one of the few things in the world that was mine and mine alone." I suck in a breath, release it slowly. "If I told anyone, if the truth came out, then it wouldn't just be mine anymore." My throat goes tight, eyes burning, and I have to push the next words out. "And if it wasn't just mine a-anymore th-then—"

God!

Why is this so hard?

Why does it feel impossible?

Atlas reaches over, and at first, I think he's just taking my hands.

Then I realize he's gently opening them, unclenching my fists, spreading my fingers, stopping me from digging my nails into my palms.

Something I hadn't even realized I was doing.

"I'm listening, Briar," he says and finally there's no edge to his words now.

They're just...Atlas. Just my big brother who's always had my back.

I nod, acknowledging that. "Thank you." And with his deep brown eyes on mine, I find with him next to me and Royal close and not annoyed that I can push through the storm cloud that is Dash...

And the rest of the words come a little easier.

"The truth is that Colt is Frankie's father."

Atlas's hands tighten around mine.

Royal curses softly under his breath and sits back.

Dash...well, when I look up at my brother, he's still. Beyond still. So fucking still he could be a statue.

Until he explodes into motion.

"Fuck!" he shouts, bursting out of his chair.

He doesn't storm out of the Sapphire Room, doesn't leave.

Instead, he picks up the chair he was sitting in and launches it —*launches* it—across the room.

It explodes, pieces of wood and splinters flying in all directions.

Thankfully, no one was standing where he threw it, but that's all I have to be thankful for because a heartbeat later, he's grabbed my arms and yanked me to my feet, both of his big hands coming to my shoulders.

"Are you fucking kidding me?" he growls. "Are you—?"

"Don't," Atlas says, stepping between us, and my heart skips a beat when Royal tucks me close to him. "You don't *ever* put your hands on a woman in anger."

"She—"

"I know what she fucking said," he grits out then says, "but still fucking *never*."

Dash inhales, exhales. Then nods tersely at Atlas before his eyes come to mine.

They're still angry, but now that anger is banked.

"I'm sorry, Thorny," he murmurs.

I slip out of Royal's hold, move over to him. "I know," I whisper. "I should have told you."

"Yes, you should have," Royal says.

Turning toward him, I open my mouth, to say what, I'm not even sure at this point—because what else is there to say? But before I can get that far, another voice joins the conversation.

"This isn't on Briar," Colt says, stepping out of the shadows.

He's here.

Of course he is.

And Dash goes still again.

Fuck.

Talk about terrible timing.

That still only lasts a second before Dash is in Colt's face, his big hand gripping the collar of Colt's tee.

Colt doesn't react, doesn't try to pull away, doesn't do anything but stand there as Dash growls, "You fucked my sister!"

"No," he says quietly, evenly, still not shoving Dash away, still not reacting to the pissed-off male grabbing him by the throat. "I made love to the woman I was falling for."

"You fucked her and then you fucked her over by leaving."

Now Colt starts to react, anger bleeding into the lines of his face. "I had every intention of coming back."

"Right," Dash mutters. "Same as you were planning on seeing Lindsay Donovan again. And Becky Connors. And Stephanie McDougal. And—"

"Shut the fuck up." He rips Dash's hand off him. "Briar was nothing like them and you know it."

"I don't know *anything!*" Dash shouts. "One second you were dead, and now you're alive. One minute you were gone, and the next I'm finding out that you fucked my goddamned *sister.*"

Not going to lie, hearing Dash recount Colt's former lovers doesn't feel great.

But neither does what happens next.

Colt shoves Dash.

And Dash shoves him back.

I gasp, thinking about those broken bones, the still-healing cuts, the fading bruises.

"Fuck," Atlas snaps. "Dash, calm down. Colt, sit your ass down before you fall over."

Royal takes a step toward them, as though to corral them.

Too late.

Dash throws a punch.

Colt takes it, then throws one back.

And then...they're fighting.

And it's brutal and intense and scary and...I react without thinking.

"Stop!" I cry as I launch myself between them.

Something that is supremely stupid.

Because I've never been in a fist fight, certainly never in one that involves two people who have been trained with deadly skill.

And I've thrown myself in the middle of them.

Right as Dash looses a right hook toward Colt's head...

I see his face change, watch as he tries to stop.

Feel Colt's arm come around my middle, trying to pull me back.

But there's no fighting physics, not when strength and momentum are on its side.

My brother's fist glances off my temple, and I go down with a cry, pain exploding on my face. I know it's a glancing blow, Dash trying to stop, Colt dragging me back, but God, that hurts a fucking lot.

And they were punching each other over and over again, nothing about the blows glancing in the least.

"Thorny," Dash whispers, crouching in front of me, his face full of regret. "Let me see."

I shake my head, hand over my throbbing face. "No, I'm fine," I say. "You need to stop with Colt. He's hurt and—"

"Here." I look up, see Atlas is holding out a bag of ice. "On your face. Now."

"Honey, I'm so sorry," Dash says. "I didn't mean—"

"I know."

"You need to go," Atlas snaps. "Get your fucking head together before someone else gets hurt."

The look on Dash's face.

Dammit, it *hurts*.

"Thorny," he whispers again.

"Just go, Dash," I tell him softly. "Listen to Atlas. Go and calm down, and when you're ready we'll talk."

He clenches his jaw tightly together. I know he doesn't want to go.

But I also know that *he* knows he's totally fucked this up.

So, a moment later, he's gone.

A moment after that, I give in to the tears burning my eyes.

And a moment after *that*, Colt lifts me into his arms.

"B-but you're h-hurt—"

"Shut it, baby," he orders and then holds me closer, holds me like I'm the most precious piece of treasure in the world.

And then he carries me out to my car.

Sixteen

Colt

Last night went so much worse than I anticipated, but my gut told me I needed to be there. Nothing that goes on between me and the boys has anything to do with Briar —outside of the fact that we all love her.

The bond Dash and I share—shared, I guess—is something that's hard to explain. I was close to all of them, but Dash and me... with the military bond on top of the hockey bond on top of the shitty family bond on top of the Gamebreakers bond was... special. We really did consider ourselves family. Brothers.

When we were in Afghanistan, we were inseparable. Every mission, every duty shift, every basketball game or video call home —we shared it all. About the only thing we never shared was a woman.

And my attraction to Briar, well... it wasn't black and white.

When I first met her, she was a kid. A teenager with braces and Coke-bottle lens glasses. She was cute in the way you look at a family member, but not sexually attractive to me. However, that gave me the opportunity to get to know her. The real Briar. Inside and out. Her hopes and dreams, her fears, her romanticized wish

—the way only a sad teenager can portray—for a family of her own one day that wouldn't be *anything* like the one she grew up with.

By the time she got rid of the glasses and grew into her curves and figured out how to tame her wild hair, we were already close. And even though I was deployed for most of her time in college, I watched her grow. Change. Mature.

When we were home on leave, she and I spent a lot of time together, both with the boys and without. Nothing ever happened back then, but I liked hanging out with her. Even her friends in college were cool. Smart. Funny. Not completely absorbed in partying—not like I had been.

I knew she had a crush on me. She didn't even try to pretend. She would say things like, "someday you're going to realize the puck bunnies and military bunnies will never understand you like I do." I'm not sure what a military bunny is, but I got her point.

Because she was right. But I always brushed it off without making her feel bad. I knew Dash and the others would go postal if I touched her, so I pushed those feelings way down to a place where I thought they would wither and die.

That never happened.

Somewhere along the way I realized my feelings were changing. Growing. The letters she wrote me while I was deployed were personal. *Private.* Not ones I shared with Dash. Not because there was anything going on, but because I knew one day there would be. At some point, I stopped fighting the inevitable.

Then the black ops group came calling.

That changed almost everything, but there was no universe where I gave her up. I just had to come up with a plan.

That weekend before I was supposed to leave for my training, before I really understood what I was getting into, we met for breakfast. I needed to talk to her about my feelings and she was the only one who knew I'd decided to stay in the military, even though that wasn't a completely accurate description of the job I'd taken.

Again, I was operating on the idea that it was safer for my family and friends if they didn't know what I was up to.

But Briar was different.

I trusted her in a way I couldn't trust the others. Mostly because she wouldn't try to talk me out of it.

One thing led to another, feelings were confessed, and it was the best thirty-six hours of my life.

And now... fuck.

Now everything is spiraling.

The house is quiet and empty, with Briar at work and Frankie at school

I roam the hallways and bedrooms like a ghost, trying to find my place, both here and with my friends. Royal and Banks, we're going to be okay. What I did couldn't hurt them the way it hurt Dash, and Atlas by extension. Atlas and I had a strange connection. Both of us had mothers who didn't want us.

My phone buzzes in my pocket, startling me out of my dark thoughts.

Igor.

"Hey, man." I walk outside to take the call, staring out at the beautiful landscaping without really seeing it.

"How are you?" he asks in his barely discernible Russian accent.

"Physically on the mend. Everything else... shit."

"What happened? Your girl find someone else?"

"I wish that was the only issue," I admit grudgingly.

"Oh, boy. What's up?"

"The boys—especially Dash—are pissed. Because there's been a plot twist you don't know about."

"Yeah?"

"I'm a father."

"Briar had your baby?" Igor probably heard more about Briar while I was delirious than someone should.

"She's four, Igor. Four fucking years old. She'll be five in February. She had her while I was still in training."

He mutters a string of Russian curses.

"Right?" I'm almost fluent now, which is weird but also comfortable, so I switch languages. "And she has a boyfriend."

"Are you going to kill him?" He switches back to English.

"I don't think so," I admit. "He seems to adore her. Treats her well. Is very gentle with her. Exactly the kind of guy she *should* be with."

There's an extended pause before he says, "What the fuck are you talking about, Colt?"

Anger I wasn't expecting.

"Huh?"

"What do you mean 'the kind of guy she should be with'? You know that kind of guy she should be with? A guy like you—no, wait... exactly like you. Because it should be you!"

I laugh, even though the reality of my situation is in no way funny.

"And what if she doesn't love me anymore?" I counter. "Or, she loves me, but isn't *in* love with me, the way she was before I left?"

"That might be the case, but you can't know that if you've been pussy-footing around. That's your woman. And your kid! Are you really going to just walk away and let her ride off into the motherfucking sunset with some other guy? Seriously?"

"It's not nearly that simple." I tell him about last night.

"Is she hurt?" he asks automatically.

"No, not really. She might have a little bruise, but to be fair, Dash pulled back the moment he saw her move, so it wasn't even close to the hit it would have been. And I saw it coming, so I managed to get her away before it could do any serious damage."

More Russian muttering.

"He didn't mean it. The punch was intended for me. She literally jumped between us. I'm going to have to have a chat with her about her need to protect me."

He's quiet again. "A woman who isn't in love won't jump

into a fist fight between two men who are literally capable of killing with their bare hands."

Fuck, but I want that to be true.

"You have to fight for your family," he continues. "I mean, isn't that why you left the agency? Your country spent a lot of time, money, and resources training you—and you walked away. If you aren't going back, why aren't you fighting for the people you left it for?"

I get up and start to pace, ignoring the tugging in my side and the stiffness in my knees.

Carrying Briar to the car the other night set back my recovery, but I wasn't going to let anyone else put their hands on her and... it doesn't change what's really bothering me.

"I don't know if my family wants me back," I admit.

"Bullshit. People don't get upset when they don't care."

"That's what I thought about how angry Dash was to find out I was alive. The things he said about me sleeping with his sister...well, that shit cut deep. It's a separate issue from me coming back from the dead."

"What about the other guys?" he asks.

"From what Briar said, Banks had guessed. Frankie's eyes— her name is Frankie, by the way, named after my dad—"

"That's nice," he says softly.

"Yeah." I pause to gather my thoughts. "Anyway, Banks had guessed because her eyes are literally just like mine. Hair color too. And he's okay with it. Royal seemed surprised but not mad because it's obvious Briar and I had something real back then, if not now. Atlas was furious but you know how he gets—all stoic and pensive, like he has to *decide* how to react."

Igor chuckles.

Igor played with us in college, so he remembers what they're like.

"Then you start with them. Make sure they understand your plan to buy a ring as soon as your training was over. How you were *in love* with her. How you waited because you didn't want to disrespect them, but you couldn't deny your feelings anymore. All that nonsense."

"Have you ever been in love?" I ask after a moment.

He's quiet for a beat. "I have. Which is why I know what I just said is some romantic sappy shit, but she's worth it, no?"

"She's worth everything."

"Then act like it."

Seventeen

Briar

I inhale and brace before pushing through the door.

I've been avoiding this all week, ever since the confrontation at The Sapphire Room and I still don't want to be here tonight.

But I also know that I need to do this.

Need to smooth things over with Dash.

And considering I was the one who told him to go, I know he's going to give me time and space until I reach out.

So...I'm reaching out.

Partly because it's killing me to have this gulf between us.

He's my big brother. He's always had my back, has always looked out for me.

I hate the idea of him hurting because of something I've done.

No, I don't think he's been reasonable about anything regarding Colt since he reappeared in our lives almost two weeks ago now.

But I also know that he took Colt's death harder than the rest of the guys.

Then adding in the secret of Colt being Frankie's dad...

Yes, I was frustrated and my feelings were hurt, but I understood he was right there with me too.

Is right there with me.

And the other part of the reason I'm here today is because Willow called to gently—in her sweet, kind way—tell me that aside from the hurt and frustration and the betrayal, Dash is also feeling guilty as hell about hitting me.

That was an hour ago.

Now, I'm here.

And I would have been here sooner if not for L.A. traffic.

If it had happened before—if Dash had hurt me before—I might feel differently. But he hasn't ever been the type of big brother to put his hands on me, not even when we were kids. More like hover beneath me when I was doing the monkey bars and cyberstalking my college dates.

A.K.A. smothering me with protective instincts.

Which is why I'm here.

We're going to settle this so we can move forward.

No more raging out. No more fist fights.

No more stress and dissension and throwing chairs.

Our family is finally together again.

We're not going to be torn apart.

Nodding sharply to myself, I use my keycard to unlock the door, turn the knob and push into Dash's security office.

It's quiet, most of the desks in the large open space empty, the computers shut down for the night. Some of his employees are out in the field, acting as personal security for the rich and famous in SoCal. Others are traveling with Dash's clients as they work on location, shooting music videos, movies, or commercials, providing bodyguard services wherever the need is.

A lucky few are in a tropical location, escorts as the client vacations.

And several unlucky fellows—the ones still at their desks this late in the evening—are watching security feeds.

Boring as hell.

But probably one of the most important aspects of the services Dash provides.

Because they don't do full twenty-four hour a day monitoring unless someone is in danger.

So, those watching the screens need to be on top of their game.

They are—or Dash wouldn't have hired them.

Dash, whom I can see from my position just inside the door, is pacing back and forth in his office, phone pressed to his ear.

Stressed.

Frustrated.

And this shit between us isn't helping.

I wave at the guys scouring those monitors then head to Dash's office, knocking at the glass door.

He spins around, a scowl on his face.

Then freezes, his expression smoothing out.

I point to the door, silently asking if I can come in, and he unsticks, nodding rapidly, moving toward me.

But the time I'm pushing inside his office, he's hung up the phone, shoved it in his pocket, and met me three feet from the threshold.

"Thorny," he whispers, his voice raspy with emotion, regret etched into his face.

I don't make him wait any longer.

I throw myself into his arms.

He catches me—as I knew he would—and holds me tight. I don't miss that his lungs hitch before he buries his face in my hair, saying, "Fuck, Briar, I'm so damned sorry." He pulls back, cupping my jaw in one big hand, gently turning my head from side to side.

The tiny bruise I had faded days ago, but that doesn't stop him from smoothing his thumb over the spot, from pressing his lips there.

"You're good, Dash," I whisper. "*We're* good."

"I hit you," he mutters, dropping his hands and pacing away from me. "I'm such a dick."

"Was it my favorite thing?" I say, moving toward him. "No. But it was an accident, and it's done now."

"I *hit* you."

Damn.

He really is beating himself up.

"I shouldn't have walked into the fray. That was dumb."

"It was," he says, shoving a hand through his hair. "But I still hit you."

"You did. But you also hit Colt, who is injured and recovering from being in a Russian prison for four years."

His face screws up into a scowl. "The bastard deserved it."

"Dash," I warn.

"He left us, made us think he was dead"—his scowl deepens —"and he fucked my baby sister."

Right, I'd breached the gulf, but he's seriously pissing me off.

"It wasn't like that," I snap, "and you know it."

"What I know is the man who was supposed to be my best friend, betrayed me. *Huge.* Twice."

"Can I punch *you* this time?" I say, and it's half-sarcastic, but only half. Because the rest of me wants to shake some sense into him.

He rolls his eyes.

I take a deep breath, shove down my temper.

"Look," I say. "I wasn't a child when Colt and I got together."

"You were still too young."

Breathe. Don't murder your brother.

"Dash, please."

He stares at me for a long moment, and I swear to God, I can see him mentally crossing his arms, even if he doesn't do it on the outside.

Still, I keep trying.

I have to. It's *Dash.*

"We fought the attraction for a long time," I say. "And you

know he fought it for longer. I wasn't very sly about keeping my crush hidden and by the time I was old enough—"

He snorts, but I ignore it.

"By the time I was old enough to be with Colt in that way, we were on more equal ground. We were close friends and that grew into something deeper, something special."

"If it was something so special, why'd you hide it?" he asks recalcitrantly.

"Because you're acting like this." I sigh. "If he was alive and you found out, we'd be exactly here, but I thought he was gone, honey. And you're Dash and he was Colt, I didn't need to do anything to tarnish that memory."

I pause, waiting for him to reply, to meet me at least part way.

Unfortunately, he just keeps scowling at me.

"So, we're here," I say quietly.

A terse nod. "We're here."

"Are you going to hold on to this grudge so long, you're going to alienate yourself from me?" Something flickers across his face, and I push. "From Frankie?"

Silence, long and tense.

Then he exhales and I finally see some of the stubborn fade away.

"No," he mutters, "I'm not going anywhere."

Relief pours through me. "Good."

"But I need a little time to sort this shit through."

"I can give you that, big bro," I say softly.

We hug, and then, disappointed but not hopeless, knowing that time is the least I can allow him, I let him walk me to my car.

I'm just turning onto my street when my cell rings.

I jab at the screen. "Hello?"

"Hey, baby."

I still, lungs hitching. Then murmur, "Hey, West. How are you?"

He fills me in on the road trip. I tell him the latest with the family and Frankie.

It's not easy, not like it normally is.

There are too many pauses, and I stumble over Colt's name more than once.

Just a hiccup, I know.

We'll get back to normal.

"I should probably go," I say after I sit parked in my garage, my car still running for a solid five minutes.

"Are you and Frankie still coming to the game tomorrow?"

Right. The game I promised both West and Frankie we'd be at.

The game I forgot about because my life is a shitshow.

"Yeah," I tell him softly. "We'll be there."

He pauses, long enough that I think I've lost him.

But before I can ask if he's still there, his voice comes back on.

"Is Colt coming too?"

I suck in a breath. "Is—would that be okay with you?"

Another pause. Then, "Of course. You're my girlfriend, and he's Frankie's dad and Banks's friend. We should spend some time together."

"Oh," I whisper. "Right."

"I trust you, baby."

The thing is...

What if I don't trust myself?

Eighteen

Colt

The last week has felt like a God damn eternity.

Living with Briar but not being able to touch her, be with her the way I want to, is a whole other level of torture. What makes it harder is the gap between me and the boys. Banks is fine, just busy with the team. Royal is okay too, but I feel the emotional distance between us because, no matter how we try to mask it, it's not the same.

I'm not the same and none of them are the same, so it was stupid of me to come back hoping it would be.

Things will shift back into some semblance of normal—whatever the fuck that is. It's just going to take time and I've already lost so much, it's hard to have patience. But I need to. Both because my family is important and because I'm not giving up on Briar. She might be dating West but there isn't a whole lot going on right now. No sleepovers, no trips, no sweet, romantic phone calls. Nothing.

Not that I'm privy to her private conversations, but she's either home or at work. A lot. And I know for sure she's not sleeping at his place. If I were him, and she were mine, there isn't a chance in hell I'd be keeping a polite distance while she lives with another guy. No, there's more going on here and I'm not giving up until I've proven to her that I'm the man she's always wanted me to be.

Tonight, we're going to a Vipers game.

All of us.

Frankie has been talking about it non-stop. Uncle Atlas's private box. How Auntie Lily and Auntie Jade sometimes sing the National Anthem. How baby Maisie gets to go too, with special little headphones to protect her from the noise. It's adorable, if not a little exhausting.

"She's at that age," Briar murmurs as we get to the arena and park in a VIP section. Frankie has barely stopped talking long enough to take a breath or let us answer her questions.

"All day?" I ask with a faint grimace.

She chuckles. "Sometimes."

I nod. "You think we could buy her something to eat?"

She laughs. "That will work for about ninety seconds."

I scoop Frankie up as we walk toward the entrance, a little annoyed that she's wearing West's jersey, but that's the least of my worries. According to Briar, she has five jerseys, and she rotates through them, including two of Banks's, a generic away jersey, and West's. Must be nice to be four and have friends and family who are professional hockey players.

"There's Uncle Banks!" she yells as we walk down to the ice.

Banks grins in her direction, nudges West and another guy on the team, Magnus Forsberg, and they head for the glass. West scoops up a puck, points to Frankie and tosses it over the glass. I lift her higher so she can grab it, and she holds it to her chest like she just reached the pot of gold at the end of the fucking rainbow.

"Yay!" She wiggles in my arms, pressing one hand against the glass and grinning at West, who grins back.

Fuck. Me.

I hate every second of this, but I have to tamp down the anger and jealousy and frustration and allow my daughter to revel in the attention—and the love. I don't care who it comes from, love is love, and all kids need it in spades. God knows, I didn't have a single iota of it after I lost my dad.

After a few minutes of the guys making faces at her and joking around, we finally head toward the elevators that lead to the private boxes. Briar has to show a special pass just to get on, and an attendant takes us up there.

It's quieter up here, yet no less exciting, and the moment we get to Atlas's box Frankie wriggles out of my arms and runs to his.

"Uncle Atlas—look!" She holds up her puck and Atlas leans down to scoop her up.

"That's pretty cool," he says solemnly. "I'm pretty sure I don't have one of those. Not even Uncle Banks's."

She frowns, and then holds it out. "Would you like it?" she asks softly. "Uncle West can give me another one."

"Oh, baby, no. That one is yours." His face softens and he presses a kiss on her forehead. "If I really wanted one, I'd ask Uncle Banks."

She wraps her arms around his neck. "But I want you to have one too!"

"That's sweet, honey." He hugs her tightly, his eyes closed, as if this little girl is the only thing in the world that matters.

I don't miss the irony because she should be the only thing in the world that matters—especially to me. Obviously, her mother is in a class of her own, but Frankie is my kid. My daughter. A baby I never dreamed of but always wanted. The plan in my head had been to get through training while giving Briar that year to establish herself professionally. Then we would get married, and I'd be able to give her the general details of my job. So she wouldn't worry. Well, so she wouldn't worry *as much.*

You're always going to worry when your significant other has a dangerous job.

At some point, when both of us were somewhat settled in our careers, we'd talk about a baby. Or three or four. I was a sad, miserable only child, physically and verbally abused by both my mother and the subsequent string of stepfathers.

There was no one to protect me or have my back until I met the guys in college.

I wanted what I had with the guys for my future kids.

Now I have one, but she calls me Colt instead of Daddy. Not even Uncle Colt, just Colt. Like I'm one of her mother's random friends. And it stings.

I'm working on it, though.

And I won't give up until they both love me.

But the only jersey I want to see my kid in is Banks's.

"Hey." Atlas nods in my direction once Frankie runs over to see Maisie.

"Hi." I want to crack a joke or say something about how much I love seeing his relationship with Frankie, but I'm suddenly tongue-tied. He's one of my best friends in the world and I don't know how to talk to him anymore. He wasn't a billionaire the last time I saw him.

"How are you feeling?" he asks politely.

God, this really sucks. This is the equivalent of talking about the weather.

"I'm better," I say. "It's been slow going. I have to see a nephrologist on Tuesday, so he can test my kidney function."

I was hoping for a smidge of sympathy, and it worked—I see the concern in his eyes.

"It was that bad?" He pauses and then slowly lifts his hands in an almost helpless gesture, which is so out of character for him. "I guess I don't know what happened to you."

I nod. "You could have asked."

His eyes meet mine and—finally—I see the smallest hint of regret.

Maybe we're getting somewhere.

"I could have," he says. "But you threw a double whammy at us."

"I didn't mean to. To be fair, I had no idea Frankie existed. I thought my superiors were forwarding my mail while I was in training. And it wasn't until I got back last month that I found out I'd been declared dead. If there was any possible way for me to get in touch, I would have. You have to believe that, Atlas."

There it is, me laying it on the line with as much brutal honesty as I can muster up.

He stands there, studying my face, as if trying to wrap his head around it.

"You were in Russia," he says after a moment.

"Siberia."

He grimaces. "Jesus."

"Four years. Daily beatings. Torture. Minimal food. Cold and hungry every day." I take a breath. "I don't want sympathy—I just want you to understand that there isn't a force on this earth that would have willingly taken me away from Briar and the rest of you. I fought like hell to survive so I could get back to all of you."

Another long, calculating beat of silence.

He stares, and I stare back.

I've never been afraid of my brothers, and after what I've been through, there isn't much that scares me. About the only thing that strikes fear in my heart is the thought of losing my family. Briar. Frankie. The boys.

Everything else, even a deadly glare from the shrewdest businessman in the world, is nothing but a glancing blow.

"I need time," he says finally, putting his hands in his pockets. "To get right with...everything. You and Briar—"

"I love her now and I loved her then," I respond bluntly. "I fought it. She fought it. We did our best to play by the unwritten rules you guys set up. But we couldn't. And just before I left, we laid everything on the line. I was going to marry her, man. There was no bullshit hooking up going on. She was never a conquest or a notch in my bedpost. Briar and me—it was the real deal." I glance over to where she's laughing with Aspen and Lily, and for a moment neither of us speaks.

"She's with West," he says. "For the first time since... well, since you died, she's finally happy. Don't come in here, mess that up, and then go chasing whatever high you were after five years ago."

I shake my head firmly. "That's done. I quit and I'm not going back. You have my word, Atlas. I'll never hurt her—or any of you —again." I extend my hand—and wait.

He looks down at it hesitantly.

Then, ever so slowly, he puts his hand in mine. "I still need a little time."

"I understand."

"Welcome home, brother."

Fuck, but that feels good.

NINETEEN

BRIAR

"And then Magnus walked out, and his entire car was wrapped in plastic."

"No, it wasn't," I say, setting my wineglass on the table.

He grins, and I can't deny it's a wonderful smile, one that used to make my heart skip a beat.

Now...I like it.

Like it a lot—that he smiles easily and laughs often, that he shares and is sweet and patient and open with me.

But now I can't help but feel like something's changed.

Because the thing I let go, the person I said goodbye to is currently occupying my guest room.

Mentally groaning because that thought—along with the guilt it's so joyfully wrapped in—is completely unwelcome. Especially right now, especially when West and I have finally been able to make up for our canceled date.

During the season, his schedule is shit.

Mine is always busy, what with Frankie and work and travel.

But now Colt is back, and I don't have to do it on my own—

or do it on my own as much as Dash, Atlas, Royal, Banks, and the girls had ever allowed me to.

It's different with Colt, though.

There's no guilt, not like I battle when the guys and girls watch her. He's Frankie's dad and they're settling in slowly together and they need to make up for lost time.

But part of me wonders if that's really why I'm so comfortable.

Or if it's just because Colt and I have started to settle back into our old selves.

Meals together.

Talking about everything and nothing.

Sharing looks across the dinner table that only we can decipher, slipping back into inside jokes and quiet smiles and—

"Earth to Briar," I hear and jerk.

Realize I've been staring into my wineglass like it holds the key to the universe, tracing the bottom of it—around and around the circle of glass.

"Sorry," I say, deliberately shoving Colt and all the complications he brings me out of my mind. "I was thinking about how many rolls of plastic wrap it would take to cover Magnus's car."

His mouth tips up. "Scuttlebutt says it was only five."

"Five?" I pick up my glass, take a sip. "I was thinking it would be more like thirty."

"Apparently those rolls go a long way."

I grin at him. "Good to know."

"Planning something?"

"You never know when you might need to plastic wrap a car."

"Don't forget the Vaseline?"

I pause, wineglass poised on my lips. "Um, excuse me?"

He chuckles. "They put Vaseline all over his windshield, baby. Apparently, it was a pain in the ass to clean off. So," he reaches across the table, laces his fingers with mine, "if you're planning teenage-esque antics, make sure to add Vaseline to the shopping list."

"Another thing that's good to know."

He winks at me then lifts the bottle from the table, takes my glass, and tops it off.

We've finished eating, a delicious meal of Caesar salad (West) and minestrone soup (me), pasta for our mains (fettuccini alfredo for me and pesto for him) with loads of homemade focaccia, and tiramisu for both of us for dessert.

I'm stuffed.

I'm slightly buzzed.

West insisted on paying even though, like always, I've offered to treat him—or at least pay my fair share.

And, like always, he wouldn't hear of that.

So, *like always*, I gave in.

"I missed you," I whisper.

He stills for a heartbeat then sets the empty bottle down and looks over at me. "You've had an eventful couple of weeks."

I squeeze his hand. "I'm not the only one. The road trip, home games and all those extra practices..."

"Yeah," he agrees and then his face goes gentle in a way that has my heart squeezing. "And I missed you too, baby." He picks up my glass, passes it to me. "But now we're back here. Together. So, tell me what drama is happening at work while we finish our wine."

The drama this week is far less old flames reappearing from the dead, and more...

Contract negotiations and meeting after meeting after *meeting*.

But at least that means I manage to come up with a funny story about Atlas scooting in late to one of those meetings.

With bright red lipstick on his collar.

"Being with Lily agrees with him," West says.

"You're not wrong."

I've never seen Atlas happier.

Or working this little.

It's a good thing—for him to finally have balance.

We talk more as we finish our wine, and that, at least, is like it's always been with West.

Easy and fun and enjoyable.

But then our glasses are empty and he's helping me push back my chair, holding my coat for me to slip my arms into.

"I don't know if I told you, baby, but you look beautiful tonight," he murmurs as we walk to his car.

I glance up at him. "You did tell me." I touch his cheek. "But thank you again."

A wink. "Thank *you* for giving me that view."

His eyes drag down my body and I can't lie.

It responds back.

Heat blooming in my middle as I drift closer to him.

West is hot. West is a great kisser.

West has an incredible physique.

I shiver, thinking about all the incredible things we've done with his incredible physique...even though we haven't quite gone *there* yet.

Not with the busy schedules and the four-year-old and my need to take things slow.

That shiver catches West's notice, and he's bundled me into the passenger seat of his car only a few moments later, the butt warmer on, the heater blasting as we head out of the restaurant parking lot.

All because he thought I was cold.

God, he's such a good guy.

And I'm—

"Baby?"

"Hmm?"

"Are we heading to your place or mine?" It's a casual question, a careful one.

As though he's bracing himself for my answer.

My stomach twists.

Because I want to say his place—want to prove to him that he's the only man I'm thinking about, the only man I yearn for.

But the twist proves that's not true.

Because...

The thought of going to West's place while Colt is at home...

I *can't.*

"It's been a long week."

Those were the words I was thinking, but *he's* the one who says them out loud.

God, I hate that he can read me so clearly.

Almost as much as I hate what I'm feeling right at this moment.

Guilt.

So much damned guilt.

It sits heavy on my chest, stifling the easy conversation from earlier, and by the time he parks in the driveway and walks me up to my front door, I'm having a hard time drawing in a full breath.

I need to get my head straight.

I *need* to put Colt behind me so I can move on with my life.

Or maybe I need to let West go so he can move on with his?

Or—

Knuckles running lightly over my cheek. "Make sure you get some sleep tonight, honey."

"I will," I whisper. "Thanks for a great night."

His mouth curves. "Anytime, baby."

Then he bends down to kiss me...

Right as the front door swings open.

With Colt standing on the threshold.

TWENTY

COLT

I t's a dick move. I know it, and anyone I tell this story to will know it—but there's no way in hell I'm going to watch my woman kiss another man. Technically, she can kiss anyone she wants. I'm well aware of that. I simply can't let it happen.

So, I wave to West with as friendly a smile as I can muster up. Watch as Briar says something to him that makes him laugh. Watch her kiss him—right on the lips—and then storm past me into the house.

She has every right to be mad but that's too bad.

"What the fuck was that?" she snaps, whirling on me the second I lock the door behind us.

"What was what?" I ask innocently. "I heard a car in the driveway."

"Don't fucking bullshit me!" She's really mad—eyes blazing, chest heaving, hands on her hips.

The problem is that it's hot. In fact, there's nothing hotter than Briar when she's furious. Her eyes turn a color I can't even name, consisting of swirls of green and gold and yellow. It's so fucking beautiful I can't resist pressing my lips to hers.

But I'm only able to enjoy a tiny taste because...she's *really* mad.

"Knock it off!" She shoves me back. "I'm with West—I told you that! I'd never cheat on anyone. Certainly not with you!"

Ouch.

That little barb stings.

I can't let it deter me, though. She's the only woman for me, so giving up is not an option. No matter how mad she gets.

"I waited until it was too late last time," I reply simply. "I'm not doing that again."

Another blindingly furious glare. "Waited for *what*, exactly? Your turn? Because you're not even in the running this time, buddy!" She heads for the stairs, but I grab her arm, pulling her back to me.

"When they were torturing me, it was your face, your touch— the memories of our night together—that gave me the strength to keep going. To keep fighting so I would *get* another chance."

Her eyes fill with tears, but she takes a step back, slowly shaking her head. "I can't do this with you again, Colt. I'm sorry." She stomps off into the kitchen and I let her go this time.

It isn't supposed to be this complicated. In my head, she waited for me. I know that's unrealistic—I was dead—but I didn't know that until a couple of weeks ago. For four years I envisioned a tearful, *joyful*, reunion.

Instead, my girl has a pro hockey player boyfriend, my closest friend in the world hates me, and I spend as much time trying to win over my four-year-old as I do my girl. Frankly, it's exhausting. If just one thing could be easy, it would be great.

I hear the sliding glass door lock disengage, slide open, and then close again.

She always goes outside when she needs to think, so I give her a few minutes as I grab a beer and attempt to clear my head.

This is going to be an uphill battle. I know that now. But I've weathered much tougher storms than Thorny Briar. So, I need to pull up those figurative big-boy pants and go talk her off the ledge.

When she was a teenager, they called me the Briar Whisperer because I was the only one who could reason with her. Dash was too blunt for a hormonal sixteen-year-old, and she walked all over Banks. Royal didn't have the patience, and Atlas kept her at a distance in the beginning, unsure how to interact with a girl her age.

So, I would be the one to ask about the boy she liked or the teacher who was giving her a hard time. Whether it was in person or on the phone, I could always make her laugh. Even back then, when I still looked at her like a kid, we could talk about everything.

Maybe my best move at this point is to go back to the beginning.

"Hey." I join her outside and sit across from her. "Want to talk?"

She fixes a fiery look of annoyance in my direction. "What could we possibly have to talk about at this point?"

I pause.

She has a point.

'Want to fuck?' probably isn't the right direction to go.

But conversation was never an issue for us.

"Watch any good TV lately?" I ask, like it's the most normal thing in the world.

She's quiet for a beat, studying my face. I watch the annoyance turn to weariness and weariness turn to...mischief.

"Welp, you've got five seasons of Law & Order: SVU to catch up on."

"That's still going? Jesus. Captain Benson in charge these days?"

"Oh, yeah."

"She was always a badass."

"She still is. She has a kid now. I don't know if she got him before you left?"

"Yeah... he was the baby of a hooker or something, right?"

"Yeah. Now he's about thirteen. They aged him up."

"I guess I have a lot to catch up on."

"And Dancing with the Stars is still going."

That was our secret guilty pleasure—the guys would have castrated me if they knew I not only watched it but enjoyed it.

"Is it still good?"

She tells me about the new professional dancers on the show, which have been her favorite performances, and then she looks up a few on her phone, showing them to me. Before long, I've slid onto the little love seat next to her. Our heads are close together, her left side pressed against my right.

Briar and me.

Me and Briar.

Sitting together essentially watching TV—just like we used to. Before I was deployed, I would sit in my room in my apartment—her in her dorm room—and we'd watch things together on nights neither of us had anything to do.

Fuck, I've missed this.

Her laugh.

The way she puts her hand on my thigh without realizing she's done it.

And I don't move, don't touch her, don't say or do anything to break the spell.

"Want another beer?" she asks.

I hate that she's moving but I nod. "Sure."

She goes back into the house, and I breathe deeply. I'm so hungry for her touch it's driving me insane, but I have to take one baby step at a time. Both with her and with Frankie.

Tonight was the first time I gave Frankie a bath. Briar told me to play it by ear when it came to bath time. Banks, Royal and Atlas have all stopped doing it now that she's a little older and the girls are happy to step in. Dash still does if he has to, but he's started to back off too.

"You're her *father*," Briar explained quietly. "If she's uncomfortable, that's one thing, but if you'd been here all along, you would have been doing everything I do. Just like I would still be bathing a four-year-old boy, if we'd had one. She can do most of it, but I don't leave her alone more than a minute, like if I have to grab something, and then I have to wash and rinse her hair because she doesn't get all the soap out..."

So, when it came time for her bath, I kept things simple. "Is it okay if I help with your bath tonight?" I'd asked.

She stared at me for a long beat and then shrugged. "I guess so. But I want bubbles."

Briar had warned me that bubbles always turned into a huge ordeal, and to proceed with caution, but for my first time I figured it might make things better for both of us. And it had gone without a hitch. A messy hitch—bubbles fucking everywhere—but it turned into a bonding moment, where I was almost as wet as she was by the end.

I look up when Briar comes back out, taking the proffered beer. "Thanks."

"Sure." She sinks down next to me again without hesitation, but now she's staring up at the night sky. "Remember Tijuana?" she whispers.

I chuckle. "I do."

She'd begged to come with us one Christmas when we'd come home from college. The plan was to go party but we had to behave if we brought Briar. Eventually, we relented and she was completely mesmerized by it all, both the good and the bad. The street vendors. Restaurant employees standing outside the bars offering two-dollar-shots of tequila.

"First time I ever got so drunk I puked."

"Dash was pissed."

"I know." She giggles. "It was hilarious watching him glare at every single person who dared to look at me. But I had a blast."

"I did too."

"Because of you," she whispers after a moment. "You kept Dash from ruining my night, and whenever you were worried we might be in a dangerous spot, you'd put your hand at the small of my back, like we were together. So, I pretended we were, and that it was a date, instead of a night out with my brothers."

"I wasn't there yet," I admit. "Not then. But that's around the time I started to realize you weren't a kid anymore."

"You knew, you just weren't ready to admit it to yourself yet. Otherwise, you would have just put me in the middle of the five of you. Instead, you found a way to touch me that wouldn't alert the others to your feelings."

If that was the case, I don't remember it that way, but she's probably right. She usually is.

"Remember the Frozen Four Championship in Buffalo?" I take a pull of my beer as she throws her head back and laughs.

"The one time my parents made an effort to show interest in Dash and hockey." She shakes her head. "We got that freak March blizzard, and they couldn't leave town for two days and they were *soooo* mad."

"Meanwhile, bad influence that I am, I was sneaking you shots of Goldschlager."

She laughs. "While sledding down that hill at two in the morning!"

I grin. "Fucking epic."

"Atlas wiped out, and he had to walk all the way up the hill again."

"He was so pissed..."

She rests her head on the cushion, so she's looking up at the sky. "We had so much fun. Sometimes I miss those days. Before life got complicated."

"Same." I lie back so we're in the same position, staring up at the stars.

"You cold, Briar?"

"A little."

I slide my arm around her, and she doesn't protest, merely nestles against my side and continues to look up at the stars.

"I missed you," she whispers in a tiny voice.

"I missed you too, baby."

TWENTY-ONE

BRIAR

I smile at West from across his kitchen table.

He smiles back.

Silence—something that's not been unusual tonight, but something that's seriously *un*usual with West and me in general—falls.

Typically, it's easy with West.

Conversation flows and it's not a struggle to find things to relate about.

Hockey and work, funny stories with the team and drama at the office. Frankie's latest Frankieisms and the fact that the young kids on the Vipers don't know what a floppy disk is.

Tonight isn't that.

I don't know what it is—or maybe I don't want to allow myself to accept what it is.

But deep down I know. With so much certainty it's filling the room.

And I'm not so naive as to think that West hasn't picked up on it too.

He took one look at my face when he answered the door then leaned in and kissed me on the forehead.

Then hugged me tightly.

No words. Just West.

And...cue guilt.

For sitting with Colt late into the night, for talking about TV shows and old memories and then...falling asleep pressed against him.

It felt so right, reclined on the loveseat, the world quiet and dark around us.

Not fighting. Just talking. Just us being Colt and Briar again.

If I'm being completely truthful, it was like coming home.

Finally feeling like myself again after all these years.

Meanwhile, I'd just come from a date with the man sitting across from me, the man who's been patient and kind and sweet and not at all an asshole about my baby daddy returned from the dead who's living in my house.

God, West really deserves so much better.

"Thank you for cooking," I say softly.

He studies me with eyes that see far too much. "It's not a problem, sweetheart."

See? He's so damned nice.

"Right," I whisper, focusing back on the plate of homemade pasta.

Yup.

Homemade pasta.

And garlic bread.

That's not homemade—the bread at least. The garlic deliciousness he spread on top of it before putting it in the broiler to get all golden-brown and crispy and yummy is, though.

And he made his own Caesar dressing too.

Something that's also delicious.

He's clearly putting in the effort.

Showing me this time with me means something to him.

The worst part is that it means something to me too.

Which is why this is so freaking hard.

I scoop up a forkful of pasta, but I don't lift it to my mouth—or I *can't* because I feel like I might throw up.

Clink.

My eyes fly up and I see West has dropped his fork to his plate.

Before I can ask him what's wrong, he pushes his chair back, rounds the table, and takes my hand, drawing me up from my seat.

"Wh—?"

But he doesn't speak, just drops his head and kisses me.

It's a great kiss—his lips are firm, his tongue is sure as it darts into my mouth, his arms are strong, his body flush against mine...

And yet, it's so *totally* wrong.

He pulls back the moment those words drift through my head.

"Yeah," he murmurs. "I knew it."

I press my hand to my chest, heart sinking, stomach twisting. "Knew what?"

His eyes close and he releases me, turning away, hands settling on the island, and when his head drops, shoulders slumping, I *know.*

"West," I whisper.

He's still for a long moment. Then his head lifts and his eyes lock onto mine.

And God, the pain in them *hurts,* almost as much as his words.

"I felt it the moment I walked into Sunday Dinner." A breath, his big body shuddering. "But I knew it when I saw the way you looked at him when he held Frankie up to grab a puck."

I suck in a breath, a tear slipping down my cheek.

"You looked like a family."

Fuck.

My lungs hitch, and I shake my head. "I didn't— *We* didn't— Nothing's happened—" A sob escapes. "West, I promise you nothing has happened between us. I'm with you—"

"No, honey," he whispers, "you're not."

Hand pressing harder against my chest, I step back...

And stumble.

But he's there, steadying me before I can fall.

Of course he is.

Because West is such a good guy.

"I know nothing's happened," he murmurs, drawing me close, hugging me tight. "Because you're Briar. Because you're sitting across from me, eating your favorite meal, and you're tearing yourself apart, baby. I'm falling for you—no, I *fell* for you a long while back."

"I—"

He lightly presses his thumb to my lips. "I know you were right there with me. I *know*. But he's the one for you. He's Frankie's dad. He's *Colt,* and I can never, ever compete with that."

Said with blunt, heartbreaking honesty.

Another sob escapes, and I bury my face in his chest.

"*West,*" I whisper.

His hand settles on the back of my head, keeping me there while I try to not completely fall apart.

"I didn't want us to end like this," I say when I can manage to speak.

A light tug at my hair has my head lifting. "I know," he says gently. "But you can't turn yourself inside out trying to keep it."

I close my eyes. Breathe. Then open them again. "You deserve to be with someone who's not doing that."

"Yeah," he murmurs, but something about the way he says that has my heart convulsing.

Because I'm not sure he believes that.

"West," I begin.

He turns and starts for the hall. "Come on, sweetheart. Let's get you home."

"I can—"

His eyes hit mine, hold.

"Briar, I may not be the man who gets to show you how precious you are. But I'm the man who's driving you home."

———

As usual, instead of West making things hard, he even makes breaking up easy.

The drive is quiet, but he turns on a playlist to fill the quiet, to make it so we aren't sitting in painfully awkward silence.

And then he walks me up to the front door, touches his knuckles to my cheek, and whispers, "Be well."

Be. Well.

The only saving grace is that Colt doesn't open the door tonight.

But he's right inside the hall when I unlock and push through the entrance.

And suddenly, it all hits me.

And I'm hurt and scared and freaked out and—

"Go away," I mutter.

He lifts his hands. "I'm just getting a beer."

But he doesn't go get said beer.

Or go away.

Instead, he steps closer, face clouding. "What the fuck happened, Briar?"

"Nothing." I turn for the stairs. "I'm going to bed."

He snags my arm, drawing me to a halt, eyes molten, anger in his words. "Did he hurt you?"

Protective Mode activated.

And I just don't have the patience—or maybe the strength—to handle it.

"No," I snap. "Now go away."

He doesn't go away, of course he doesn't.

In fact, he draws me closer.

And it feels good.

Guilt ripples through me. I am such a fucking mess.

"I'm going to kill him," Colt growls.

I jerk my arm free, shove at his chest. "West didn't hurt me. If anything, *I* was the one to hurt *him.*"

"What the fuck are you talking about?"

"It's none of your business."

"Briar."

Ugh.

He's not going to let this go, and I just want to go upstairs, cry my eyes out so I can have my shit together for Frankie in the morning.

He turns gentle. "Talk to me, baby."

Gentle. I can't handle gentle right now.

Which is why I say something unforgivable.

"Why did you come home now? I was finally doing good, finally over you and moving on a-and now you've ruined everything!"

His eyes flash with anger.

And hurt.

More things to feel guilty about.

"Well," he says evenly. "I'm back and I'm not leaving."

"Well," I parrot meanly, "you're no longer welcome to do that with me."

"What the fuck are you talking about?"

"I mean," I draw out. "You're not going to be living *here*. So, we'd better figure out how to co-parent."

His eyes hold mine.

For a long, long time.

I hold his gaze right back.

"Are you fucking kidding me?"

I lift my chin. "I want you out in a week."

"You don't mean that."

"I do."

"Briar."

"I fucking *do*, Colt. All you've done is fuck everything up and I'm done being the one who has to sort through the aftermath."

His face clouds, but I don't stick around.

The guilt and hurt is choking me, and I'm about to lose it.

I can't have him around to see that.

So, I turn on my heels, sprint up the stairs, rush into my bedroom, and shut the door, leaning back against it.

Waiting.

Half expecting him to be right behind me.

Knocking.

Demanding I let him in.

But there's nothing but silence...until there's not.

Because as I'm standing there in my bedroom, heart aching, tears streaming, and feeling like I'm going to puke, I hear the front door open and close.

I hear Colt leaving.

And that's when my knees give way.

TWENTY-TWO

COLT

I t wasn't until I was outside that I realized I have nowhere to go—and no way to get there.

I don't know where Dash or the others live, and while I certainly have the skills and contacts to find out, that feels wrong given the way things are between us. I don't have any friends here in L.A. and Briar's house is pretty much the only place I've felt comfortable since I got out of the hospital.

The one thing I do have is money, so I'm thankful for that as I call an Uber to take me to the one place I'm familiar with that might have a friendly face.

The Sapphire Room.

There are perks to the training I have, like being able to sneak in and out of almost anywhere, but that feels like too much work tonight. So, I march up to the front door like I belong there.

"You're not on the list," a big, burly bouncer announces.

"My friends own this place," I say, hanging on to my patience by a thread. The last week or so has felt like an eternity. I just want to sit at a bar and drown my sorrow for a few hours. Is that too much to ask?

"I don't care if your mother owns the place," the bouncer replies with a shrug. "If you're not a member, and you're not on the list, you don't come in." He folds his arms across his massive chest, and it occurs to me I probably can't take him. Not in my current condition.

Fuck.

"Look, could you just—" I start to pull a fifty out of my wallet but then I hear a quiet, familiar voice.

"It's okay, Ernie. He's with me."

Aspen.

She has a soft, friendly if not curious, look on her face.

"Thanks," I say, following her inside.

"What are you doing here?"

"It's been a long...week."

"Then I have just what the doctor ordered." She walks behind the bar, and I can see by the bottles she grabs—she's making a Gamebreaker.

Yes. Thank fuck for little things.

I settle at the bar while she expertly makes me a drink and slides it across the bar to me.

"Thank you." I reach for some money, but she waves me off.

"Your money's no good here."

"I appreciate that." I don't know what else to say so I gulp down the drink and push it back toward her. "Am I good for another?"

"Absolutely." Her eyes twinkle as she makes the second one. Then she picks up her phone and types something.

"Don't bother calling in reinforcements," I say dryly. "None of them want to talk to me."

She chuckles. "Well, I can't speak for all of them, but I know my husband does."

Banks.

He's a good man. Different from the others. He always was. Just a laid-back guy who only cared about two things—hockey and his brothers. Everything else was background noise to him.

Royal always had a dark, serious edge—the full-on rockstar long before he made it big. Focused and ambitious, there was no doubt he was going to be a star.

Dash was a tough guy, inside and out. Got in more fights than I did, which says a lot, and won every single one. He protected Briar like it was a full-time job, to the extent that even I was a little intimidated. I didn't know how I would ever explain my feelings for her to him.

And there was Atlas. Closed-off, introverted, and academic. He was a hockey player like the rest of us, and could party hard on occasion, but his studies were important too. He had a plan and though I wasn't around to see it come to fruition, I never doubted it would.

I guess I was an oddball too. I didn't have a focus. I loved hockey, but I didn't harbor any illusions about the NHL. The military was the next logical step, but I knew early on it wouldn't be enough. There was an itch, this wild need for adventure and righting the wrongs of the world that I couldn't share with my brothers.

Deep down, I suspect that plays a part in why it's been so hard to win them over. They knew I would leave them—certainly not the way I did—but they resent the fact that I did it without giving anyone a head's up.

"I'm going to say a penny won't cover the thoughts you're having right now." Banks settles onto the bar stool next to mine.

"Probably not," I acknowledge. "Who's watching Maisie?"

"Mrs. X."

"Who's Mrs. X?"

"She's our adopted grandma. She was Aspen's neighbor before we moved in together, looked out for her. So now we're returning the favor. She lives with us as an unofficial nanny, housekeeper, grandma, or whatever else is needed. Mostly, we just love her."

I smile.

Of course they do.

That's who they are—Banks and the others.

"She sounds great," I say a little wistfully.

"You'll meet her soon enough. We want to have you over to the house."

"You got a guest room for me?"

He arches a brow. "Sure. Why? You need a place to stay?"

"Briar and I had a fight. She kicked me out, and I realized I have nowhere to go. No one to turn to."

"And you came here." He smiles. "You know this is all for you, right?"

I turn my head curiously. "This? What's this?"

"The Sapphire Room."

I'm confused. "What do you mean?"

"I mean, we bought it so we would have a place to hang out and remember you. Briar came up with the name because people used to say your eyes looked like sapphires, so...The Sapphire Room. And there's always a table reserved for you—" He swivels on his stool and points to the table where everyone was sitting the last time I was here.

For the first time, I notice the little placard that reads "Reserved for Colt."

Now my eyes feel scratchy, and an all-too-familiar wave of guilt jolts through my system.

"Don't." Banks puts a hand on my arm when I drop my head. "You should have told us your plans but even if you had, we wouldn't have known that your superiors lied about your death. That part isn't on you."

"It still feels like shit."

"I just wish you'd trusted us."

"It wasn't about trust," I respond, lifting my drink and guzzling what's left. Almost like magic, another appears, and I nod at Aspen before turning back to Banks. "If Dash knew what I was going to do, he would have followed me—and I couldn't allow it. Someone had to stay back, take care of Briar."

Banks's eyes darken. "The rest of us never would have let anything happen to her! We would have taken care of her."

"Yeah, but how would she have dealt with losing both of us? The man she was in love with *and* her brother? I knew the danger —at that point in my life, I craved it as much as I craved her. But I knew I would never be able to settle down if I didn't go out there and...do it. Save the world or whatever the fuck I thought I needed to do."

"It didn't occur to you that Briar would still be devastated by losing you?"

"Of course it did. That's the part that's hard to explain to her. But Dash kept her on such a tight leash, by the time I got my head out of my ass and figured out that I was legit falling in love with her, I'd already signed. I couldn't back out. I wrote letters while I was in training. A whole fucking year of letters... that those fuckers never sent."

Banks scowls.

"They were full of apologies to you guys and promises to Briar. All the ways I would make it up to her once I got through training. I guess in my head I compartmentalized...like, compared it to being in the military. Go to Russia, catch a bad guy, come home to my wife and family. Individual missions. They explained what it would be like, but I thought I knew better, that I could handle it, no matter what they said. Then my first mission went straight to hell in a hand basket. And now..." I down my third drink.

"You might want to slow down," Banks says dryly. "I really don't want to have to carry you home."

I chuckle. "I'll be fine. And I really need a numbing agent right now."

"Must've been a doozy with Briar."

"Yeah." I absently drum my fingers on the bar. "She doesn't want me."

"You still have feelings for her?"

I turn to him, squinting slightly. "Loving her is the only reason I'm still alive."

Banks is quiet. Watching my face. Waiting for me to continue.

But there's nothing else to say.

I love her. She doesn't love me back anymore. She's in love with some fucking douchebag hockey player who'll never love her as much as I do. He might treat her better, but no one will ever love Briar the way I do. It's simply not possible.

My silence must reflect something about my state of mind because Banks finally cocks his head.

"So, what are you going to do? Are you staying or leaving again?"

"I'm not leaving my kid," I say firmly. "I've missed too much already. I just don't know if I can watch Briar with West. That's a knife to my heart every fucking time I see them together."

He frowns. "You know they...broke up, right?"

My head snaps to the side. "What are you talking about? She came home from her date and told me I was fucking up her relationship, her life. Then she told me I had a week to find another place to live. Normally, she backpedals after we calm down, but she didn't. Not this time."

Banks glances at me, squinting. "So... you packed your duffel and just walked out?"

"I couldn't stay in the house with her that mad. I was bound to say or do something dumb. It was easier to just leave. I can get a hotel."

"No way." He shakes his head. "You'll come home with us. Mrs. X will love having another lost soul to mother. Or grandmother as the case may be."

But I'm not really listening.

I'm still focused on what he said a minute ago.

"How do you know they broke up?" I ask.

"Because we have a group text thread on the team and he sent out an SOS about an hour ago wanting to know if anyone wanted to go get wasted with him. Someone asked if Briar finally wised up and dumped him and he responded with 'the details don't matter. I just can't compete with a dead man.'" He's reading off his phone and despite the alcohol swimming in my system and the buzz making it hard to concentrate, now I understand.

That's why she was so upset.

West dumped her—what a dumbass.

But that's okay.

Because I'm right here to pick up the necessary pieces to put both our lives back together.

Twenty-Three

BRIAR

My eyes are so swollen from crying, I can barely read the words on my kindle screen.

But even if I could, the romance novel I've been reading in my spare time isn't making me feel better.

For once, getting lost in the fantasy of a man falling at my feet isn't what I want.

Because in the last couple of hours, I've hurt two good ones.

West because...well, he's not Colt.

And Colt because...he's Colt.

The Colt of my dreams, my fantasies, my heartbreak...and a different Colt who I'm still learning, who's told me things that shatter my heart all over again and then piece it back together.

And I told him to go.

When he has *nowhere* to go.

My lungs hitch and I slam my eyes closed, trying to breathe deeply. I need to stop crying. I've shed so many damned tears I should be a shriveled up skeleton by now.

But I can't seem to get them to stop.

And now I can't read, not from my swollen eyes or because

it's painful watching the main characters move toward their happily ever after, but because my vision has gone blurry.

"Ugh," I whisper, dashing away the offending tears.

I need to go to sleep.

Frankie will be up bright and early, and I've got to get ready to tell her that I...kicked her father out.

Great.

That'll be fun. Can't wait—

The door to my bedroom flies open.

I gasp, thinking that Frankie's sick or some maniac has broken into the house. But even as those thoughts are crossing my mind, I'm freezing.

Because a big hand is catching it, stopping the wooden panel from slamming into the opposite wall...

And Colt is striding into my bedroom.

I can't ignore the thrill that brings.

I just don't have all that long to process it...

Because the next second, he's swinging the door shut.

Click.

The lock goes and my breath catches.

"What are you—"

His head whips toward me, blue eyes blazing with something I can't read—or maybe it's that he has so many emotions flying through his face, I can't detangle them all.

Rage and hurt.

Need and heat.

Softness and pain.

And *yearning.*

So deep and intense it calls to that well inside me, the one that's existed from the moment this man walked out my door five years ago. One that's grown, yawning and gaping, its deep black depths reminding me that despite all I have and no matter how lucky I remind myself I am...

My life is empty.

Without this man.

Even as I'm thinking that, he starts moving again.

Toward me.

Toward my bed.

And not stopping until he's right beside it, his eyes full of that flurry of emotions but his tone deadly calm.

"You've been keeping things from me."

I clench my Kindle a little tighter, lungs suddenly constricting. "Wh-what are you talking about?"

He just stares at me for a long moment.

Then he says, "You know exactly what I'm talking about, baby."

I blink. Swallow. "Colt."

Something ripples through his eyes when I say his name, but he just murmurs, "Talk to me."

"About what?"

"Baby."

And when he doesn't go on, I start to get irritated. "About *what*, Colt?"

He just lifts a brow.

I huff out a sigh, lift my Kindle. He wants to play the silent game? Great. I can do the same *and* get lost in my fictional love story.

At least this hero won't ever leave his woman.

But I barely get my eyes on the screen before he's plucking it out of my hand and tossing it aside.

"Hey!"

"You and West?" he asks icily.

I still.

Then realize that's dumb.

That I've given away too much.

"West and I are none of your business," I tell him.

"It damn well is."

I open my mouth to snap back, but I don't get so much as a single syllable out.

Because his hands are wrapping around my wrist and he's

yanking me up to my feet and—*oh my God...*

He's kissing me.

This is insane.

He's insane.

I've spent the last hours alternating between crying myself out and engaging in enough self-flagellation that I may start turning toward BDSM.

And now the man I fell in love with as a teenager and then again as a woman is here. In my bedroom.

And he's kissing me.

I don't think.

I don't keep lashing myself with guilt, scalding my cheeks with tears.

I just...react.

My lips part and my body melts.

Colt groans, one arm banding around my middle, his other hand diving into my hair, tilting my head back and deepening the kiss. His tongue slips between my lips, sliding into my mouth, tangling with mine...

I moan.

And things explode.

My hands are ripping at his T-shirt, tugging at the hem, trying to yank it over his head.

But since he doesn't end the kiss, it just bunches up between us. Still, I take advantage of that bared skin, sliding my fingers over his torso. Hard and male.

Mine.

He tears his mouth from mine, gets rid of the tee and then he's working at my pajamas, shoving down my shorts, pulling up my tank top, tossing it to the side.

Leaving me in just my underwear.

And not a pair that covers very much.

"Baby," he rasps, his eyes dragging down the length of me— my face, my naked breasts, those skimpy panties, my legs.

Which are shaking.

"Fuck, you're beautiful."

He is too. Strong and lean and a survivor. I want to kiss the scars on his chest, make them disappear. I want to hold him, stroke him, feel him inside me. "Honey, I—"

His hand lands on the center of my chest and he pushes.

Not hard.

But hard enough I end up back in bed.

And he's climbing on top of me.

His lips find mine again, and this kiss is hot, deep, wet. *Urgent.* Our bodies out of control, needing to touch, needing to make up for lost time.

When he releases my lips, I'm grinding against his thigh, already close, moaning out his name as he kisses his way along my jaw, to my ear, flicking out his tongue, tasting the sensitive spot behind it.

I shiver.

Then I'm moaning again because he's kissing his way down my throat...and not stopping until he makes it to my breasts, cupping one, closing his lips around my nipple and—

"Colt!"

"Mmm," he groans, sucking harder, using his free hand to palm my other breast, to tease the nipple there with sweeps of his thumb.

I dive my hands into his hair, holding tight to the deep brown locks.

Keeping him against me.

Needing him close.

He switches breasts and I melt, because God that feels good.

So good that I barely notice his hand sliding down my side.

But I do notice it when his fingers dip under the waistband of my underwear.

I stiffen, a bucket of icy water pouring over me.

He feels it, stopping, lifting his head from my breast and meeting my eyes. "Baby?" he asks and it's a rasp.

I look away, shame and guilt and need warring.

His hand slips out of my underwear, comes up and cups my jaw. "Talk to me," he says gently.

I swallow hard, tears threatening again.

And I don't know if it's that I'm exhausted, if it's because it's late, or if it's because this is Colt...but I tell him the truth.

"I'm not ready for this."

Silence.

His big body going so, so still.

Then he sighs softly and rests his forehead against mine. "I know."

I blink, look up. "I'm sorry."

His eyes are gentle. Warm. "Don't ever apologize for stopping when you're uncomfortable."

"I—"

His fingers flex. "Not *ever*. You get me, baby?"

I want to bristle at the order, purely out of principle.

But his words are sweet.

And they get even sweeter when he asks,

"But does this mean you'll come to dinner with me tomorrow?"

TWENTY-FOUR

COLT

Date night.

I'm more excited than a teenage boy getting laid for the first time.

Not that I give a shit about sex—Briar and I have plenty of time for that. I just can't believe we're going out on an honest-to-goodness date.

How long have I waited for this? Six years? Maybe more?

Back then I was in Afghanistan and she was in college. She was writing me letters and that's when it really started. The letters weren't just nonsense from a giggling college girl, though there was a little of that too. Instead, they were filled with hopes and dreams—the kind I started wanting to share with her.

It wasn't black and white back then. Dash would have had my balls in a vise if I so much as hinted at something with his little sister, but it was there, simmering beneath the surface, threatening to turn into a full-blown inferno.

And the fantasy that came to mind most often was a picnic on the beach—so that's what I have planned for tonight.

We dropped Frankie off at Royal and Jade's place, and I've

just turned Briar's SUV toward the beach. Supplies are in the back, thanks to Jade, whose help I enlisted since I don't know where anything is around here.

"Are we going to the beach?" Briar asks as I head south.

"We are."

"It'll be chilly once the sun sets."

"I have blankets."

"Multiple?" She seems amused.

"One is for us to sit on. The other one is in case you get cold."

"We could have had a quiet evening at home—with unlimited blankets." Ever practical, Briar points this out.

"But then we would have been dealing with Frankie, and as crazy as I am about her, this is adult time. We need it."

"We do." Her hand slides across the center console, searching for mine. Warm fingers seeking out connection. The bond that's existed almost since day one.

"It's funny how I kind of always knew this was our destiny," I muse, knowing she'll understand what I'm trying to say.

"Even when I was a bratty teenager?"

"You were never bratty. Dash made it seem like you were because he's your brother and he didn't want to think about you as a woman, so he put you in the slot little sisters go in. It was different for me. Obviously, it took a while for the connection to make sense...for me to realize it wasn't about sex or being good friends, you know?"

"But it was," she says gently, squeezing my hand. "Because that's kind of what a relationship is, right? Having a best friend you want to have sex with?"

"I never thought of it that way, but yeah, I suppose so."

We pull up to a small, secluded beach that's almost deserted now since it's late in the day. Jade told me about it, and when I looked it up, it was perfect for what I had in mind for tonight. Nothing fancy—that's not how either of us roll, at least not often —and somewhere we can be alone.

"I've never been here," Briar says in surprise.

"Jade recommended it."

She smiles. "Of course she did."

We get everything out of the back and work together setting up. It's not cold, but the sun is starting its descent into the horizon and that means it will be soon enough. But that just gives me an excuse to hold her.

"This looks amazing," she whispers as I set out the food I picked up from the caterer Jade suggested. They specialize in picnic basket meals for romantic dates, and it's exactly how I envisioned it. Wine. The fanciest, most elegantly plated cheese and meat platter I've ever seen. Fresh bread. Chocolate-covered strawberries. I hope this is the kind of thing Briar likes.

I open the wine while she pulls out plates, napkins, and wine glasses.

The petite sirah is a brand I've never heard of, but what do I know? Most military men don't drink wine while deployed, and there certainly wasn't any in a Siberian prison. Briar recognizes the name, though.

"Oh, this is from Oak Ridge Vineyards?"

"You sound like you know them."

"I do. Atlas and Jean-Michel, the owner, are friends."

Yet another detail I know nothing about.

I must have sighed or had a weird look on my face because she leans over and runs her knuckles across my cheek. "You'll get up to speed before you know it."

"I'll never get back the years I lost," I whisper gruffly.

"No, but those were out of your control. We can't go back in time, so we focus on being more present in the future. Like you've been doing with Frankie. In a few years, she won't even remember that you didn't come into her life until she was four."

"Four and *three-quarters*," I correct solemnly.

She laughs, rolling her eyes. "Yes, let's never forget the three-quarters."

We eat and talk, conversation coming easily for once. The new client Atlas has been stringing along because he's been such a jerk.

Frankie deciding she's ready to learn cursive. *And* Mandarin since her bestie at school is Chinese.

"Let's watch the sun set," I suggest once we've done a significant amount of damage to the platters of food.

I put most of it back in the basket, then I spread my legs and hold out my arms. Briar doesn't hesitate, settling with her back against my chest like we've done it a thousand times—even though the truth is that we've *never* done it. Not like this.

So, I wrap my arms around her, pull her close, and we stare out at the setting sun without saying a word. There's a cool breeze coming in off the water, waves breaking gently on the shore, and I can't remember the last time I was this relaxed. Briar's head falls back, settling into the hollow of my shoulder, a lock of her hair rising up to tickle my face.

"This is beautiful," she whispers.

"Not as beautiful as you." I let my fingers drift to her face, gently turning her head so I can capture her lips with mine. My movements are slow, deliberate, gauging her reaction—I don't want to rush her like I did last night.

"When you kiss me...it's like there's nothing but you and me."

"There's never been anything but the two of us. Not since that night we spent together."

She twists so she can look at me, and I stare down into her gorgeous green eyes. So much fire in those emerald depths—but also passion, sincerity, and much more. All things I love about her.

I dip my head, kissing her again, this time with more intensity because I can't seem to help myself. Her mouth fuses to mine greedily, like she's been waiting for this. Lips and tongues tangle deliciously, warmth spreading over me as she presses her torso to mine. Slowly, because my sore body is protesting this awkward position, we slide down to the blanket.

I reach for the extra throw and pull it over us as we continue to kiss. And kiss. And kiss some more.

She slides a hand under my shirt, pressing it flat against my abdomen before gliding up to my chest. Warm fingers trail along my ribcage, tracing one of the more recent scars that's still healing. It feels so good, goose bumps break out on my skin. But it's not enough. I need to feel more—I need to feel everything.

Rolling onto my back, I tug her on top of me, mouths still locked. With her sprawled across me, I nudge one knee between her legs. It feels so right to have her lying on me like this, breasts firm against my chest, the heat of her core pressed against my thigh, lips pliable as I pillage her mouth.

Fuck but she feels good.

There's no way to hide my arousal so I don't even try, taking her hand and pressing it to my erection. "You feel what you're doing to me?"

"Believe me—it's the same for me."

"Can I touch you, baby?" I take a moment to search her face.

"Please." Her eyes turn to liquid fire as she caresses my cock through my sweats.

She's so God damn beautiful—sometimes it hurts to look at her. But I want to do a lot more than look.

My hands drift down to her ass, and I squeeze two incredible handfuls. She's curvy in all the right places, and I'm going to enjoy the hell out of exploring every inch of her. It may not be tonight, but it's coming and that's enough for me. Hell, this alone would be enough for me. As long as I'm winning her over, keeping her and Frankie in my life, that's all I need. Anything else is a bonus.

"God, Colt…" Her voice is a breathy whisper filled with need.

I turn us so we're on our sides facing each other, and she drags my hand to her breast. Fuck, I'm going to embarrass myself if we keep this up but there's no stopping because this time she's kissing me, one arm around my neck while the other goes back to exploring beneath my shirt.

And I return the favor.

Her breasts are large and full, bigger than I remember, and I run my thumb back and forth across her nipple. I love the way it feels as it pebbles against my finger, her breath hitching. She arches her chest against my hand, and I squeeze, kneading and caressing as I take possession of her lips.

"You wet for me, baby?"

She moans an affirmative response right into my mouth, and my cock gets even harder.

I let one hand travel south, the feel of her silky skin a poignant reminder of how much I missed her. How badly I want her. How perfect she is.

"I don't want to rush you…" I whisper.

"Shh." She pauses to meet my eyes. "Touch. Me."

That's all the encouragement I need. My fingers make short work of the button and zipper of her jeans, peeling them apart to give me better access. It's almost completely dark out and we're covered with a blanket, but I don't need to see to feel what's happening between us.

To hear her moan deep in her chest when I skim across her mound.

To feel her tilt her hips up, making it easier for me to slide my hand along the soft curls inside her panties.

To catch the way she moans, long and deep, the moment I press a finger between her delicate folds.

She's fucking dripping.

For *me*.

The slickness between her legs—and on my fingers—is almost too much.

I dip the tip of my finger into her warm, tight entrance and—

"Fuck, Colt…it's been so long." She groans, canting her hips so I can slide that finger all the way in.

This time, we moan in unison.

Fucking heaven.

"Oh…Colt!" She cries out softly, so I press a little harder, looking for the spot that will send her over the edge.

She's so tight and wet, I can't even imagine what that will feel like on my cock, but it doesn't matter because she buries her face in my neck as she clamps down around my hand. Her pussy flutters and spasms, each wave of her orgasm making her jerk against me.

That small contact is enough to send me over the edge right after her, and my only regret is that I couldn't look at her face while she came.

"Holy shit." She sounds breathless. "That was...well, it's been a long time."

"For me too," I admit, chuckling. "It didn't take much. I'm sorry if it was too quick."

"Too quick?" She nestles deeper against me, pressing kisses on my neck even though she's still got my finger trapped inside her. "That was...perfect."

"You're perfect." I lower my head and kiss her temple.

"I'm sorry I didn't do anything for you," she whispers.

"Uh, did you not feel me making a mess in my boxers? You did plenty."

There's a moment of silence that I can't quite decipher and then she starts to snicker.

"What's funny?" I ask.

"Us. Lying here on the beach, making out like teenagers. It's not like, you know, we don't have a whole *house* where we can be alone or anything..."

I laugh too. "Come on, admit it—this is more fun."

"It is."

She lifts her head, and she's smiling.

Not just a polite smile, or the one she gives her friends when she sees them. Not even the one reserved for Frankie when she does something sweet. No, this smile is different.

This smile is for me—just like her.

TWENTY-FIVE

BRIAR

I knock on the door to Atlas's office and the scowl on his face tells me he knows exactly why I'm here.

Because after several weeks with Colt now being back and after Colt and I had that date, slowly making our way back to an *us*—one that's both new because we never truly got to be an *us* before everything went wrong—and old because it's been easy to slip into the *us* we used to be...just with a side portion of kissing.

Lots and lots of kissing.

And his fingers on and in me.

Mine on and around him.

And well—

"What's up, Thorny?" Atlas calls grumpily.

I shake my head, dislodging the dreamy thought of Colt and our bedroom adventures, and focus on the problem in front of me.

That being, Atlas still acting grumpy and surly and distant with Colt.

Banks has come around.

Royal too.

Things aren't easy and perfect and exactly as they were five years ago, but progress has been made and I can see the light at the end of the tunnel.

Dash, on the other hand...

It's not going to be an easy problem to solve. Even with our talk.

Neither is the man in front of me.

Atlas is doing his grumpy billionaire scowl, but I've seen it enough over the years that it doesn't affect me.

Instead, I smile at him and step into his office, closing the door behind me.

His scowl deepens further...then further again when I move across his office and drop into the chair in front of his desk.

Then just look at him.

"I have a meeting in ten minutes," he mutters.

"No, you don't," I tell him. "It could be handled with an email, so I did, and then canceled it."

He glares at me for a long moment, muscle in his cheek flexing, before turning to his computer screen and jabbing angrily at his keyboard.

I let him stew.

For a little bit anyway.

"We need to talk."

"You're the one sitting there staring at me"—a few more jabs at the keyboard—"you need to talk to me then talk already."

My mouth hitches up.

God, I love this man.

He's always been there.

Always.

Even when it meant putting himself on the back burner.

I know that if I asked him to drop everything because I need to get home to Frankie or go to a doctor's appointment or even just to take some time for a mental health break, he would bend over backward to make that happen for me.

So, I need to fix this for him.

And for Colt.

And for me.

I've worked hard to build our family, to keep us together through all the trials and tribulations that life brings.

I'm not willing to give that up.

Which means I'm going to heal this breach.

"You're not going to like what I have to say."

"No shit," he mutters, still jabbing.

"Colt needs you," I say gently and even with that gentleness, Atlas still goes even stiffer, his scowl deepening, his jabbing growing more intense. "He needs me and Frankie and you and Banks and Royal and Dash. He needs his family."

That gets him.

I know it does.

Because the family we've built is important to him too—maybe almost as important as it is to me considering his upbringing.

He finally stops jabbing, though his scowl doesn't soften. "I don't even know what to say to him."

"What do you mean?"

A long, slow exhale. "We mourned him, Briar. Grieved him. How do we move on from that?"

I still. Because I know exactly what he's feeling.

The hurt. The anger.

But, more importantly, the knowledge that changed everything for me.

"We lost him," I murmur. "But we've been given a gift, honey. A second chance. A way to make a life—a better one—with someone we grieved so intensely that we named a bar after him and celebrated his birthday for five years even though we thought he was dead."

His expression softens, and I know that I have him—at least a little bit.

So, I keep pressing.

"He's one of us. He's our family," I remind him. "And if I can forgive him after all that went down between him and me, you guys can too."

Suddenly, his scowl is back.

And I know why.

Because Atlas is starting to agree with me.

And he doesn't like it.

I push up from the chair, round his desk, and bend to kiss his cheek, to wrap my arms around his shoulders and squeeze. "I knew you'd see it my way."

"I didn't say I agreed."

I straighten. "You didn't have to."

Then I start for the door, toss over my shoulder, "The jet's waiting for you."

"What?"

"You're flying out tonight for Lily's concert."

He blinks.

I grin.

"Lily's bringing the red lipstick."

He jerks, cheeks going the slightest bit pink.

Then...he smiles.

And, since my work here is done, I head out the door.

———

"How was school, baby?" I ask as I turn on the car and back out of my spot.

"I'm not a baby," she says pertly. "I'm four and three quarters."

My lips twitch, but I don't laugh like I want to. "Sorry to say, Frankie," I tell her. "But you'll always be my baby—even when you're old."

"Like when I'm nineteen?"

This time I do laugh.

Because...from the mouths of babes.

Nineteen is old apparently.

"Yup. Even when you're nineteen." Grinning, I make my way out of the lot, turning onto the road that will lead us home, listening as Frankie recounts her day—circle time and coloring, working on writing the number five, practicing opening and closing her lunchbox to get her ready for kindergarten next year.

No joke, my baby isn't a baby any longer.

And I'm going to miss that part of her.

And Colt missed all of it—the first smiles and the first steps, her first day of school and learning her first song with Royal, the first time she called me Mom or said "I love you" or helped me cook dinner. So many firsts that he missed.

That Frankie missed too.

My heart pulses, but I don't want to be sad, so I think about the sleepless nights and breastfeeding and diaper blowouts.

I think about being in survival mode for so long that I could barely breathe.

"Is Colt going to live with us forever?"

My fingers tighten on the steering wheel. "Would you like that?" I ask, careful to keep my tone neutral.

She falls quiet.

For so long that when I stop at a signal, my eyes flick to the rearview mirror.

She has her arms crossed and is looking out the window.

But her expression isn't angry.

She's...pondering.

So, I let her do exactly that, driving in silence until she's ready to talk.

She doesn't get there until we're turning onto our street.

"You said family always makes sure to be here for the important things." Her arms cross tighter. "And he wasn't."

That has my heart pulsing again, and I weigh my words carefully.

"He wanted to be here, baby. But the bad guys who had him made it really hard for him to get home."

"I know."

And she does know.

Both Colt and I have had several age-appropriate conversations about his captivity, trying to lay it out in simple but not scary terms.

I'm not sure we've succeeded.

Especially when she says, "What if the bad guys come again?"

I pull into the driveway, turn off the car, and meet her at her booster seat, wanting her to be able to see my face when I answer her. "The bad guys can't come here," I tell her. "They're not allowed."

She studies me closely, as though considering my answer. "Like when Josie and I say 'No Boys Allowed' at the train table?"

Laughter bubbles up in my throat, but I swallow it back.

She's asking a serious question and needs a serious answer.

"Like that, honey," I say. "Except they're so not allowed that they wouldn't even have permission to come in the front door in the first place."

"So, we're safe?"

I nod even though I decide I need to clarify that with Colt—he's back and I didn't even consider if what he endured could cross the ocean and affect our lives here.

Aside from the obvious emotional and mental load, that is.

But even as I think that, I'm helping Frankie unbuckle. "Yeah, baby," I say. "We're safe."

"'Kay!" She nods and hops down from the car.

"Do you want to talk more about it?"

A shake of her head. "Nope!"

All right then.

Smiling, I grab her things and start trailing her up to the house.

Then freeze when she says, "Colt kissed you. Josie says that means he's going to be my dad for real now."

Twenty-Six

Colt

"Are we safe, Colt?"

I've just put some monstrosity of a portable beach cabana in the back of Briar's SUV when she tosses out the question so casually it takes a second for it to register.

Slowly, I turn to her. "What do you mean?"

"Your...*associates* in Russia. Or wherever. Do they have access to you or any reason to find you?"

Shit.

I should have reassured her about that the moment I set foot in her house.

"No. Absolutely not. When they caught me, I had the ID of a totally different person—someone who doesn't even exist. And they have no reason to come after me. They know—knew—I was a spy, but they never got any useful information out of me, and the whole time I was there it was just a matter of the guards making an example out of me."

"So, it was all for nothing?" she asks softly, one hand on my arm, staring up into my face with concern.

"In the grand scheme of the spy game? Yes. A big, miserable waste of time."

"And suffering."

I manage to smile, so she doesn't see the darkness that lurks in my subconscious whenever I talk about all that. "That too."

"Get help, Colt." Her voice is a whisper as she leans up for a kiss. "For Frankie, for me, and for yourself. Promise me."

Like I could refuse her anything.

"I promise." I bend my head, capturing her sweet lips—one thing that makes all the darkness disappear. Always.

"You're kissing. *Again*." The disapproving little chirp makes us both laugh. "I thought we were going to the beach?"

"We are," I reply, scooping Frankie up and tickling her. She squeals with laughter, even as a protest escapes her. "I was just asking Mommy how many more toys we have to bring because the whole car is full!"

"It's not full!" She dramatically rolls her eyes. "But I need my water guns—put me down!" She's off like a shot and I give her mother a baleful look.

"Water guns? Really?"

She arches one brow. "What? You thought the boys weren't going to make her a tomboy?"

Yeah, that would be wishful thinking on my part.

Finally, after more bags, coolers, chairs, and toys than three people should possibly need for a day at the beach, we're on the way. It's warm for November, Indian summer hitting hard this week, so we opt to take advantage of it and have a nice day.

As a family.

Briar and I are slowly finding our way as a couple, and she and I are working together to ease me into Frankie's life too. It's taking longer than I would have liked, but I'm not stupid—moving slowly is the only way this works long-term.

It's taking even longer with the boys.

Banks and I have hung out a few times.

Royal stops by a lot under the guise of seeing Frankie, but it's about me too because the last time he came over while she was at school. He pretended he forgot but I know better.

Atlas and Dash are a lot more stubborn.

Atlas texted me the other day to ask if I was interested in having a drink one night in the near future. No date or time, just a generic invitation. Briar warned me to be nice and not tell him to fuck off, so I didn't, but I will when I see him.

What the fuck is that all about?

"If you set up the umbrella and chairs, I'll get the food," Briar says once we've arrived. "And Frankie—do not get in the water. Do you hear me?"

"I hear you!" Frankie already has a pail and three water guns, running toward the shore full speed.

"She okay on her own?" I ask worriedly.

"She's stubborn and sassy and a whole lot of other things that are sometimes difficult, but she's always good when it's a matter of safety. She'll play on the water's edge until we're ready to join her."

"Okay." I glance out at the water, pausing from jabbing the pole of the umbrella into the sand. "It's warm today but the water's choppy."

She follows my gaze. "Yeah—Frankie! Don't get in the water unless one of us is with you!"

"I *know*, Mommy!" she yells.

I bite back a laugh. "She's hilarious. How do you manage to discipline her?"

"It's not easy," she admits, brushing a lock of hair out of her eyes. "It's nice when we're all together and someone *else* can discipline her so I can walk out of the room and laugh."

"I don't know that I'll be much help to you," I say, chuckling. "Because she cracks me up."

"Me too. But you'll figure out when it's okay to let her get away with stuff and when you have to be strict. Luckily, she's a good kid. It seems to be instinctive, that she knows when she can push and when to back off. The first time I lost my shit and screamed at her she gaped at me. She was...not quite two? She tried to crawl into the hot oven."

"Jesus," I breathe, grimacing.

"I'd opened the door to put a roast in, but it was heavy so I opened it all the way, then turned to pick up the pan with both hands. In that two seconds she started to climb up and we both screamed. I managed to get her before she got burned, but I was scared. That's one of the only times I've ever shrieked like that, and it was more about getting her to pay attention than punishment. I try not to ever react that way, but it shocked her into understanding how dangerous it was. She never did anything like that again."

"I don't know how I feel about discipline," I say, meeting her eyes. "Like I can't picture yelling or spanking or anything."

She pauses from where she's spreading out the blanket. "I don't spank, but yelling? Oh, yeah. It's a thing. I don't do it often, but she gets it when I really yell. You know, the full on Frankie Marie Dash—get your little butt over here!"

We both snort out laughter.

And then it hits me.

Frankie's last name is...Dash. Not Blackwood. *Dash.*

I never thought of that before.

Briar seems to realize my train of thought at the same time.

"I couldn't give her your name without telling the boys who her father was," she says quickly.

"It's all right." I wrap an arm around her neck and tug her against my chest. "I understand. But I'd like her to have...my name. Both of you."

"One step at a time," she whispers. "Okay?"

"Absolutely. I just—" My training as a spy ingrained it in me to always be aware of my surroundings. Always. Even when my girl is in my arms at the beach. But something in my peripheral vision makes me react even before Frankie screams.

"Frankie! I'm coming!"

The large wave washed right over her, pulling her into the

water and dragging her under. Somehow, I kick off my slides as I run, splashing into the cold water, eyes scanning for her bright pink bathing suit.

A little hand comes up, body wriggling and I grab her by the wrist, yanking her up and into my arms.

"I've got you, baby. Daddy's here... you're okay."

Heart racing, tears stinging my eyes, I carry her out of the water.

"Oh my God, Frankie... what happened?" Briar meets us on the shore, wiping water out of her daughter's eyes as she coughs. "I'm going to get a blanket!" She runs back to where we're set up and I follow, Frankie still in my arms.

I sink into one of the lounge chairs, holding her tightly as she coughs and sniffles.

"You're okay, baby. Daddy's right here." I hug her so close I'm probably going to suffocate her, but it's the only way I can reassure myself she's safe.

"Daddy...I was so scared." Frankie buries her head in my chest, her little body practically fused to mine.

"I know. But I've got you. I'll always be here, Frankie."

Briar rushes over with a towel and a blanket, using one to dry us off a little and the other to wrap us both up. With Frankie's warm little body nestled against mine, I've never felt love like this before. Not even for her mother, though that's obviously a different thing. I would die for both of them, but the connection I feel to Frankie is so strong I almost can't breathe.

When I finally drag my eyes away, so I can look at Briar, hers are filled with so much emotion. Like she recognizes what I'm feeling. Because of course she does. She grew this tiny little human in her body and has been her sole caretaker for four-and-three-quarters years.

"Fuck." I say it softly, but I don't care if Frankie hears me because I can't hold back. There don't seem to be any adequate words to express how I'm feeling at this moment.

She called me Daddy.

"Daddy, I was so scared."

I'll spend the rest of my life making sure she's never scared. Not if I can help it.

"It's okay," Briar whispers, leaning over to kiss the top of Frankie's head and then press her lips to mine. "Thank you."

I give her a shaky smile. "You don't have to thank me—this is my job now. Taking care of you. Both of you."

The look she gives me shows a lot of the things neither of us have been able to vocalize. But that's okay.

Because I'm not going anywhere.

Not now, not ever again.

Twenty-Seven

BRIAR

I make short work of packing up the car, getting a month's worth of cardio schlepping all the beach shit back and cramming it into the trunk far less efficiently than Colt had on the way to the beach.

But that rogue wave really scared Frankie.

And Colt.

And me.

I don't know how he even sensed something was wrong—turning away from me in the middle of a sentence, instinct sending him down the beach before I could blink.

Then I had.

And I saw it.

The unusually large wave shooting up the shoreline, taking Frankie by surprise because it was so much bigger than the others had been where she was playing. It swept forward, dragging her under and out into the ocean between one breath and the next.

She was just...gone.

Then Colt was rushing in after her, plucking her from the frothy whitewash, the heavy wave that was churning up sand, turning the already dark and cold water into something impossible to see through.

But he had seen through it.

He had found her.

Before I even reached the water, he had Frankie in his arms and was marching up the beach.

I hadn't even had time to think.

To panic.

One second, she was gone and the next, she was safe.

Colt carrying her up the beach.

"Daddy?" I hear as we're leaving Frankie's room after giving her a bath, getting her fed, and tucking her into bed...and spending a lot of time reassuring her (and ourselves) that she's safe.

Let's just say that my daughter had plenty of ice cream and cuddle time.

"Yeah, honey?" Colt murmurs from next to me, immediately reversing course and moving back into her room.

Daddy.

That does something to my heart—settles deep, opens it wide...and I give in.

Who am I kidding?

I've been giving in from the moment Colt slipped out of the shadows.

Now seeing my daughter do the same, watching the gentle way he tucks her in, smooths back her hair...gives into her plea for him to read just one more book.

Something that definitely won't be just one more.

And...it's done.

Colt used to be the man I loved.

Now he's the one I *love.*

I close my eyes as that feeling ripples through me.

Then I exhale quietly and leave them to their moment.

I get ready for bed, knowing that Colt is going to be right beside me, that he's going to hold me close.

He's been doing that every night since he found out West and I broke up.

But tonight is going to be different.

I'm...ready.

So, I go to my dresser, pull out a nightgown I never thought I would wear—one that I bought with the man who stole my heart as a teenager and never gave it back in mind. One I knew he would love...if he was alive.

Which he wasn't.

Except he *is*.

I slip into my bathroom, wash my face and brush my teeth, then step into the shower to run my razor over my legs, my bikini line, under my armpits.

Then I lotion up, brush out my hair, spritz myself with perfume.

And through it all, I don't rush.

I have time because Frankie is going to request that he read her multiple books, and he's going to give in and read them to her. Then he'll sit with her until she drifts off.

So, I fuss with my curls and oil the ends. I make sure the tight burgundy lace clings in all the right spots.

And only when I hear the bedroom door open and close do I feel nervous.

But I just suck in a breath, hold it for a second, and exhale.

Then I step out of the bathroom.

Colt is at the side of the bed, emptying his pockets onto the nightstand, plugging in his phone. "She's out," he says. "And I only had to read three extra—"

His head lifts, words cutting off.

The look on his face...God, I'll never forget it.

Heat and desire blaze through his expression, scorch me from behind his sapphire blue eyes.

Then it all goes soft.

"God you're beautiful, baby," he rasps.

I nibble at my bottom lip, those nerves making a reappearance. "My body has changed since having Frankie."

Half of his mouth turns up. "Mine's changed too." Guilt ripples through me, and I open my mouth to apologize. But he keeps talking. "Come here, baby."

"I— Colt—"

"Fuck it," he says, prowling toward me. "I'll go to you."

And he does.

One moment, he's across the room. The next, he's right in front of me.

He doesn't speak, just runs his hands reverently over my body —down my arms, my side, my hips, pausing where the material bisects my thighs, then back up my front, dragging the material with them, slowly baring my skin, inch by inch by *inch*.

His eyes are fixed on me as he pulls it free, drops it to the floor behind us, and my breath hitches. Because the heat is back, growing in intensity until it's the fiery blue inferno.

And I willingly jump into the flames.

I grab the hem of his T-shirt, tugging it up, drawing it over his head, tossing it aside.

He's beautiful.

He's mine.

And he's been hurt again and again.

"What did they do to you?" I whisper, my fingers and lips and tongue gently stroking over the pink scars on his chest, his belly.

"It doesn't matter."

I freeze, glance up, mouth opening to tell him it very much matters.

He keeps talking before I can.

"Because I could lose myself in the memories of you," he says and even as I'm sitting in the beauty of those words, he's moving, lifting me into his arms and carrying me to the bed. "You were in every thought, every dream, every fantasy I held tight to. And with you in my head, my heart, I wasn't there."

He sets me on the bed, crawls over the top of me, my legs instinctively parting so he can settle himself between them.

"Instead, in my head I was here." He brushes his lips over my forehead, my cheeks, my nose. "Right here, baby."

I exhale shakily, reaching up to touch his jaw, the bristles there abrading my fingertips in the best possible way. He presses his mouth to my palm, face soft in that way that settles deep, his eyes that gorgeous inferno, his body hard and lean and still regaining strength, but still the most beautiful thing I've ever seen in my life.

"I'm falling in love with you," I whisper.

Soft. Scorching. *Mine.*

"I've been in love with you for five years."

Another thing to settle deep, another memory to hold tight to.

And when he kisses me, he gives me more.

Our mouths sealed together, tongues sleek darts, our lips moving in perfect sync.

When it feels as though I'm going to pass out, he kisses his way to my ear, laving at the lobe and making me shiver. Then his lips are dragging down my throat, softly pressing against my collarbone.

He's gentle, worshiping me.

Touching me as if I'm the most precious object in the universe.

And I touch him right back, smoothing my hands over his back and torso, dipping into his hair and holding him to me when he makes his way to my breasts, kissing them, scraping his stubble along their undersides, gently taking my nipples into his mouth and suckling slowly and lazily.

It's unhurried, as though we have all the time in the world.

And maybe we do.

Because when he's spent long minutes lavishing attention on my breasts and is kissing his way down my stomach, lips tracing over each of the silvery stretch marks left over from my pregnancy, I'm not in any hurry.

Except to touch him, to hold him, to feel his hair on my skin and his hands pushing my legs wide and his mouth going in between.

Except to let him slowly bring me up to the precipice of an orgasm, to keep me there for long moments, both of us fighting the fall, knowing that this moment can't last forever, but wanting to draw it out for as long as possible.

So, I don't beg him for release when he gently kisses the inside of my thigh, I just touch his jaw and murmur, "Now, honey."

His eyes on mine, holding.

Then he nods, slips out of his pants, and slowly comes back over the top of me, his long, lean body the sweetest type of weight.

He braces himself on one elbow and kisses me.

Kisses me long and wet and deep.

Then, when he lets me breathe again, I whisper again, "Now, honey."

A flare in those deep blue eyes. "You sure?"

I nod, repeat. "*Now.*"

And then he's pushing inside, doing it slow and steady and unhurried. He's big and it's been a long time and he's spent long minutes worshipping every inch of me.

Which means it doesn't take long for me to be close again.

For his deep, sure thrusts to be sending me right up to the edge again.

"Colt," I whisper.

Sweat is gleaming on his forehead, his eyes burn into mine, and his breathing is hitching in a way that tells me he's right there with me. "Fuck, you feel good, baby."

"Right back at you, handsome."

He groans, settles his forehead against mine and keeps stroking into me.

"I love you," I whisper.

His eyes close.

His strokes speed up.

His hand comes between my legs, thumb brushing my clit and—

Then I'm *there*—bursting into a thousand pieces, trusting that the man inside my heart and body will catch them all, will keep them safe.

And when I emerge, safe and sound...

I do the same for him.

Twenty-Eight

S oft, steady breaths.

Choppy breathing.

Yup. Definitely two people in this room with me.

I open one eye and there she is, my favorite four-year-old. I immediately hear her voice in my head, correcting me—four and three quarters!—and I smile to myself.

"Good morning," I say.

"What are you guys doing?" she asks, frowning.

Is this a trick question?

Before I can come up with an appropriate response Briar's eyes pop open, and instead of the warmth, love, and passion from last night, I see and feel immediate tension.

Crap. What's that about?

Are kids not supposed to see their parents in bed together? Maybe not when they're not married? I don't know but I need to find out and I can't do that while I'm naked in the same room as my kid. So, I make a circle motion with my forefinger.

"Turn around, kiddo."

"You have to put your pants on *again*?!" She whirls, hands on her hips, muttering under her breath, and I manage not to laugh as I grab my sweats and Briar reaches for a robe. "Mommy, do we have time to cuddle?"

"Not today." Briar's tone is gruff, unlike her.

"Go into the kitchen and decide what you want for breakfast, Frankie," I say gently. "We'll be right out."

"Fine." Frankie glances back over her shoulder, narrows in on me—like the fact that there's no time to cuddle is somehow *my* fault—and then disappears out the door and down the hallway, her feet making little pitter-patter sounds until they fade away.

"Good morning, beautiful." I follow Briar into the bathroom.

"Morning." She doesn't turn around but leans her back against my front, allowing me to slide an arm around her waist, press kisses along the side of her neck.

"You okay?"

"Mm hm." Then she busies herself at the sink, reaching for her toothbrush. A gentle but poignant dismissal. Since my stuff isn't in her bathroom, and I need to clean up too, I simply kiss her and smile.

"I'll meet you in the kitchen."

"Okay."

I take care of business in record time, but Briar still beats me to the kitchen, looking pretty damn refreshed and awake for someone who was up half the night cuddling and whispering with me.

Frankie's up on her stool, helping Briar unload and put away everything from the dishwasher, and I stand there watching for a moment. Taking it all in.

Fuck, this was supposed to be my life while I was rotting away in that damn prison.

My beautiful girls, including the one I didn't know existed until a month ago.

I never imagined a life as incredible as the one I'm currently living. It's so much better than anything I wrote in my letters to Briar or the fantasies that kept me alive while I was imprisoned.

There is no national pride or call to serve that's stronger than what I feel watching my girls together, here in...*our* house. Realistically, I'm still a guest, but I'm doing everything in my power to change that. To become a staple in both their lives.

I don't know what I'm going to do for money going forward —the amount I made the last five years is hefty—but I'm only thirty-one. I can't support a family, put a kid or two through college, *and* have enough to retire with what I have. Which means finding a job.

All I know is it won't be as a spy.

I am *never* leaving my girls again.

Except one of my girls is uneasy this morning. Posture rigid, movements jerky, interactions with Frankie short and terse.

Something is bothering her, and I'm not going to let whatever it is fester. If I did something wrong, or pushed her too far, I need to know. Find a way to fix it.

"Frankie, would you run to my room and find my brown socks?"

I don't own a pair of brown socks.

"Okay!" She takes off like a shot, and I feel a moment of guilt for duping her, but she'll find regular socks in five seconds, and I need more than that to talk to Briar.

"Babe." I still the movement of her arms, holding them gently with my hands. "Look at me."

She freezes, but then turns slowly.

"What's wrong?" I ask quietly. "Did I do something you didn't want me to do last night?"

Eyes wide, she continues to stare at me for a beat. "We didn't use...protection."

"We didn't..." I pause in confusion. "You're not on anything?"

Flare of irritation. "I never had any reason to *be* on anything."

"You and West weren't using protection?" I ask in shock.

"Not that it's any of your business," she shoots back, "but West and I didn't have sex. It never got that far. Not with him, not with anyone else."

"You didn't..." A million scenarios race through my mind but there's something niggling at the edge of my psyche. An idea that —*holy shit*. Did she subconsciously wait for me despite believing I was dead? Did she...really do that?

Fuck, I love this woman.

"I haven't been with anyone since you either," I say quietly, so she understands she's not alone in this.

"You haven't..." She stares, blinking a few times, as if she's finding it hard to believe.

"Well, there was a strict curfew during training and then it's not like a Siberian prison is big on romance. At least, not for straight guys."

"Oh." Her expression softens, her eyes suddenly a little teary. "*Colt.*"

"Don't cry, baby." I brush a tear away with my thumb. "You know how I feel about you. I knew you were it for me, so as long as I was alive, there wasn't going to be anyone else." I shake my head in frustration. "Of course, you'd know that if you'd gotten the damn letters. I wrote to you every week while I was in training, telling you how I felt, making plans for us...I didn't know they weren't sending them. I'm so fucking pissed about that."

"Do you still have them?" she asks after a moment.

"I do. They're in a box somewhere back in D.C."

"I'd like to read them sometime."

"I can have someone send them." I brush my knuckles along her cheek. "Don't worry about anything, baby. I'll take care of protection going forward, but no matter what happens, I'm not going anywhere. We'll deal with anything and everything together. Because I love you too."

For the first time today, her smile hits her eyes and she's just leaning up for a kiss when Frankie storms back into the kitchen.

"Daddy! You don't *have* any brown socks!"

"They must be in the laundry," I reply solemnly. "Sorry about that. Did you bring me white ones?"

She proffers a pair of white—the only color I currently own—socks.

"Thanks, sweetie. Now you need to eat some breakfast."

"Are you both taking me to school today?" She looks from me to her mother.

"Do you want us to?" I ask.

I've been trying to let her guide our progress as father and daughter, so she doesn't feel pushed or uncomfortable. My sudden appearance in her life has to be jarring, so Briar suggested we let her decide when she's ready to take the next step. Like her impulsively calling me Daddy yesterday.

That was one of the greatest moments of my entire fucking life.

And now—

"You should come, Daddy. So you can meet my friends." Her eyes sparkle with excitement.

Briar glances at me. "It's a good idea for you to meet her teachers, learn the routine. I'll put your name on the approved pick-up list while we're there too. Otherwise, security is probably tighter than a Siberian prison."

Her eyes twinkle—I'm so glad she's comfortable enough to joke about what happened to me, because I refuse to let it impact my life going forward—and my chest squeezes with happiness.

I love everything about this. About them.

Ten years ago, the boys and I would have died laughing imagining a scenario like this. Me and the woman in my life taking our four-year-old to preschool. Together. Like it's a two-person job.

But twenty-one-year-old me had no idea what this future was going to look like. And in a way, I'm glad. I wouldn't have wanted to know how much I was going to love Briar because then I might not appreciate it as much as I do.

As we're walking out to the car, I snake an arm around her

waist and draw her back, whispering in her ear, "What are the chances of you calling in sick today?"

She smiles up at me, batting her eyelashes playfully. "They're pretty good if we stop for condoms on the way home."

Twenty-Nine

BRIAR

I whisk the Béarnaise sauce so vigorously that my arm feels as though it's going to fall off.

But I can't stop whisking, not if I want my sauce to survive.

And seriously, what had I been thinking, making a Béarnaise sauce to go with the carefully seared and roasted with lots and lots of butter and garlic and thyme steaks. Steaks are now resting, cooked to a precise medium rare (thanks, meat thermometer). Steaks that will accompany the scalloped potatoes. Oh, and the huge Caesar salad and roasted brussels sprouts that I threw together to accompany Colt's favorite meal.

And to get some vegetables into my family.

Our arteries will thank us.

Dessert is chilling in the fridge, an intricate chocolate lasagna.

Also Colt's favorite dessert.

I'll be serving it with huge hunks of lemon pie.

Colt's second favorite dessert.

Yeah, I may have gone a bit overboard.

But Atlas is coming to dinner (Lily is on the road), along with Royal and Jade, Banks and Aspen and Maisie, and Willow.

And...Dash.

Mostly because Willow forced him to come.

But also because I asked—or well, made it a Mandatory Sunday Dinner.

Then gave Dash my sad, little sister, puppy dog eyes to get him to agree to attend.

So, everything has to go perfectly.

Because if it doesn't then my family—

"That looks good."

I jump as Colt's voice comes from very near my ear, realize I've stopped stirring.

And now my Béarnaise is at risk of breaking.

Shit.

I whisk more vigorously, ignoring Colt when he sweeps the hair off my nape, bending to brush my lips against the now-exposed skin, making me shiver, threatening to break my focus.

"I need to finish this," I tell him, continuing to stir, but doing it as I'm sidestepping his big, tempting, *hard* body.

So I can focus.

His hand settles on my waist, and he draws me back against him, lips at my ear now. "Baby—"

I jerk when the timer on the oven goes, sparing one more look at my sauce before pulling it off the heat. It looks perfect, so I exhale a relieved breath, set it aside, turn off the burner, then hurry over to the oven.

"Baby—"

Colt is close again as I open the oven door, both of us getting a face full of steam.

I study the top of the scalloped potatoes, seeing it's almost perfectly golden brown.

Just a few more minutes.

I bend, check on the asparagus, getting more steam before I study the stalks.

Almost there. I reset the timer.

"Briar, baby—"

I close the oven door, hurry back over to my sauce and start transferring it into the serving dish.

"Briar—"

"Out," I say, jerking my chin to the hall. "I need to finish before everyone gets here."

He opens his mouth again, but Frankie beats him to the punch.

And immediately throws me right under the bus.

"Mommy only cooks like this when she's nervous."

Ugh.

Why did I have kids?

His eyes come to mine then he crouches, smoothing back Frankie's hair. "Will you go watch for your aunts and uncles, baby?"

"'Kay!" she agrees for once.

Then again, she loves her aunts and uncles.

I focus on dressing the salad, ignoring Colt's footsteps as he comes closer again.

"It's going to be okay," he murmurs, hugging me from behind and resting his chin on my shoulder as I add the croutons and parmesan cheese then finish tossing the salad.

"Of course, it's going to be okay," I lie.

Unless the men get into a fight and overturn the table, thus ruining the food and injuring Colt when he's finally almost better.

"Baby."

The timer goes off and I hurry back over to the scalloped potatoes, the asparagus, then slide in the rolls that just need to be toasted.

He waits until I close the oven then tugs me close again, cupping my jaw and tilting my head up. "Talk to me."

It's an order.

But I can tell by his set expression that he's not going to let this go.

"Dash is coming."

"I know, baby."

"He..." I nibble at my bottom lip. "He might not be... welcoming."

Colt stills.

Then drops his head back and laughs.

It's loud and beautiful and so much like the Colt I fell in love with as a teenager that I freeze, watching him, soaking it in.

His gaze comes to mine, grin wide, and then he loops an arm around my middle and drops his lips to mine.

"I can handle it, baby," he says once he's kissed me senseless.

"Ugh!" I hear from behind him, turning to see Frankie standing in the opening, Banks holding Maisie, Aspen and Jade arm-in-arm, Willow at their side, Atlas and Royal behind them, and...

Dash.

Standing slightly removed, looking ready to murder Colt for daring to touch me, to kiss me, to hold me close.

That's when the timer for the rolls goes off.

———

"And that was the end of that," Colt finishes, the story of him, Dash, and their squadron battling against a goat who was obsessed with a soccer ball of all things.

Frankie laughs, and I'm right there with her.

The image of the goat chasing them all, wanting to get the ball and not afraid to use his horns to make it happen has all of us laughing.

All except Dash.

Who snorts and rolls his eyes, shoving his food around on his plate but not really eating it.

Even though he loves my Béarnaise sauce and seared steak and scalloped potatoes almost as much as Colt does.

Not tonight, though.

I swear he's barely had a single bite.

"And then what'd you do, Daddy?" Frankie asks. "After the ball popped?"

"Well," he says, ignoring the way my brother goes ramrod stiff at her use of the name *Daddy* (something we all take his lead on and do the same), "then your Uncle Dash did what he does best."

Frankie tilts her head to the side in silent question.

Colt looks at Dash, holding my brother's gaze for the first time. "He found a way to get over it."

The table takes a collective breath, bracing.

"Then he helped me fix it."

Frankie frowns. "But I thought Uncle Atlas's superpower is fixing things?"

"It is, sweetie," Jade says.

"Even all of Uncle Atlas's fixing superpowers couldn't fix this fucked-up shit," Dash mutters from next to me.

I toss my napkin down onto my plate, turn to glare at my brother.

Willow steps in before I blow my stack, leaning over and ruffling Frankie's hair. "Uncle Atlas is great at fixing things. But"—she grins, stage whispering—"Uncle Dash is pretty good at it too."

"Oh." She considers that. "He did help me put the batteries in my remote control car."

"Because her *Daddy* wasn't around to help with it."

Another mutter.

One I hear. One that almost everyone hears.

Except for Frankie, thankfully.

Because she's gotten up to get her remote control car.

"See?" she exclaims, running back and shoving it in Willow's face. "It goes really fast."

Willow smiles, glances over at me, teeth nibbling at her

bottom lip. Then she looks at Frankie again. "Will you show me how fast it can go?"

"We gotta do it in the front yard," Frankie says solemnly. "The grass in the back yard is too thick."

"Let's do it," Willow says. "I need to walk off all that good food anyway to make room for dessert."

"Yay!" Frankie yells, running out of the room.

Willow follows at a far more sedate pace, pausing only to squeeze my shoulder. "Breathe, honey," she whispers.

I cover her hand with mine.

Then nod.

She smiles then slips from the room.

I wait until I hear the front door open and close then turn to Dash. "You're out of line and you need to stop."

"What you need to do is stop pretending you three are just a happy family," Dash grits out, spinning in his chair, his angry face close to mine, his hazel eyes flashing.

"We're not pretending. We're trying to figure things out and it's not perfect, but it's making me and Frankie *and* Colt happy so you need to deal."

"You need to protect yourself," he grits out.

"From what?" I snap, throwing my hands up. "The man who loves me?"

"From when he leaves you again!" he growls. "Because that's what he does. He fucking leaves and doesn't give a shit about the fucked-up disaster that he leaves behind!"

I flinch.

Because it's me he's talking about.

I'm the fucked-up disaster that was left behind.

Atlas opens his mouth. Banks shifts in his chair. Royal starts to stand.

But Colt is faster than any of them, stabbing his finger in Dash's direction. "You. Me. Back yard." A beat. "*Now.*"

THIRTY

COLT

Briar can be quick when she wants to be, but I'm quicker.

"No," I say gently when she grabs my arm. "He and I have to work this out."

"But you're still healing," she whispers worriedly.

"I'm fine. Trust me. And stay here." I lightly press my lips to hers and then stalk outside in the direction Dash went.

I really fucking hate this, but I'm done. One way or another, this has to be settled. I would hate for him to not be in our lives but no one—not even one of my brothers—is going to keep me from my woman and my kid. Period.

"Whatever the fuck is going on with you, it needs to end now. Today." I approach him without hesitation. He's wider than I am, but I'm taller and faster. At least, I used to be faster.

"You don't get to tell me how to feel," Dash snarls.

"I don't," I agree, "but *you* don't get to make Briar feel like she has to choose because I promise you—she'll choose me." That's kind of a dick thing to say but he has to get past this. Somehow, some way, he has to realize she and I are a package deal.

His nostrils flare and he glares at me. "The fuck she will."

"Dude. She loves me, and I love her. And I'm. Not. Leaving. I love both of them, more than my own life, so whatever needs to happen for you to let this go, then do it."

"Be careful what you wish for."

"What? You need to take a swing? Go for it. But then it's done."

Dash scowls, his face taut with tension as we stare each other down.

I'm not afraid of him but I'm also not back to one hundred percent yet—he could probably hurt me if he wanted to. Maybe. I'm still pretty tough.

It's hard to tell what he's thinking, the expression on his face shrouded but intense.

Finally, he lets out a long, put-upon sigh, the tension seeming to drain from his large frame as he says, "Fine."

I'm not stupid—I know what's coming, so I brace myself as he throws a punch that glances off my jaw.

Jesus, he's still got the hardest right hook I've ever taken from anyone.

But I don't react, don't move, barely breathe...merely continue standing there, watching him. Waiting.

"You feel better?" I ask blandly. "We done now?"

Dash takes a step closer, his body taut again. "*No.*"

Then he yanks me into a hug that nearly suffocates me.

"What the fuck, man? Why didn't you tell me you were going back in?" he growls against my ear.

"Because you would have followed me—and somebody had to stay here to take care of Briar."

My words seem to penetrate something deep inside him because he slowly pulls away and stares at me. Long and hard. Like he can't quite believe it's me, that I'm really here.

"You still should have talked to me, let me know the plan."

"You wouldn't have listened," I reply. "We were attached at the hip. And with that kind of danger, we couldn't both go in."

"You left her... *pregnant.*"

"I didn't know—I swear on Frankie's life, I had no idea she was pregnant."

He stares at me, a contemplative expression on his face.

"You have to believe I would've done things differently if I had known," I continue.

He hesitates but then nods. "Yeah, I do know."

Thank fuck.

"Fuck, it's good to have you back," he says quietly, pulling me in for another hug.

"It's good to be back," I gasp, trying to breathe through the pain of my sore ribs.

"Sniff, sniff, you two are so sweet I'm getting a cavity." Atlas is standing off to the side, smirking.

"Fuck off," Dash and I mutter at the same time in the same tone of voice.

"Oh, crap, the terror twins are back," Royal groans.

He and Banks are out here too and the five of us stand there for a moment, no one moving. It's weird but comfortable at the same time. We've hung out a million times before, but it's never been quite so...poignant.

"Should we sit?" I ask when the silence stretches out.

"Let's do that," Banks says, dropping into one of the lawn chairs.

"What do you need, Colt?" Atlas asks when we've all settled around the propane-fueled fire pit. "Money? A place to stay? A job?"

"Nah, I'm good. I was very well-paid while I was in that prison camp. And funny story—there's not a hell of a lot to buy in a Siberian prison commissary."

Dash kicks my leg. "Smartass."

"*That's* never gonna change," I say, chuckling.

"We're serious," Banks interjects, leaning forward. "What do you need?"

"Actually, taking me to get a phone would be nice at this point. This burner I've been using is really the worst."

"What, the spy world powers that be couldn't give you a regular fucking phone?" Dash asks.

"Guess I wasn't high enough on the food chain," I quip.

"I can add you to my plan," Atlas says, pulling out his phone and typing something in. "You have a preference in color?"

"Color?" I ask blankly.

"The latest version comes in cobalt blue, blackout black, titanium silver, and burning red." He doesn't even look up.

"Uh, black is fine," I say.

"Okay." He taps away for another minute and then puts his phone away. "It'll be here tomorrow. I expedited shipping."

"I can pay for the phone," I say quickly.

He arches his brows. "Seriously? After all you went through in that prison? Let me buy you a fucking phone. You'll buy your next one."

It's on the tip of my tongue to protest, because Atlas wasn't a billionaire before I left for Russia. But he is now, and the look on his face brooks no argument.

So, I give in graciously.

"Thank you," I say. "I appreciate it."

"Are you, uh, going to be living here?" Dash asks cautiously.

I turn to him. "I am. You got a problem with that?"

"Nooo." He draws out the word. "But they need stability, you know? You can't just bounce in and out of their lives."

"I already told you I have no plans to do that," I snap. "And before you say something else to piss me off—yes, I plan to marry her. But we need a little time to get our feet under us, if that's okay with you."

"Yeah, I'm good." He slowly holds out his fist.

Extending the proverbial olive branch.

I hesitate before bumping mine against it.

He's as solid and loyal as they come, but he can be the most stubborn man alive if you get on his bad side.

"You planning to work?" Atlas asks, ignoring us.

"Eventually. I'm good short-term. I want to take some time to heal both physically and mentally, focus on whatever Briar needs, and get to know my daughter."

"And then?" Dash asks, his expression inscrutable.

"I don't know. Why? You have a suggestion?"

He shrugs. "I can always use someone with your skill set at my company."

"I don't even know what your company is exactly," I admit. "But when the time is right, we can definitely talk about it."

"When's the last time you played hockey?" Banks asks me.

I can't help it—I burst out laughing.

"As cold as it is in Siberia, they do not have an ice rink at the prison."

"We could get you suited up when you're ready," Atlas says. "We rent the ice and try to play once or twice a month."

"That sounds great."

I lean back, looking around at the faces of the four men who mean so much to me. Most of my thoughts in prison were about Briar but not all of them. I also held on to memories of the good times we had. College hockey. Parties. Holidays spent with the family we created for ourselves.

Those were the things I clung to when I was sure I wouldn't survive much longer.

My brothers.

The woman I loved.

Family.

And now I'm getting a second chance with all of it.

One I don't intend to blow.

"You looked way too serious just now," Dash says under his breath.

"Just taking it all in. Appreciating it."

He nods. "Good. Because you won't get another second chance."

"I won't need one."

"Whatever you two are whispering about," Royal says, "knock it off. Since when do we have secrets?"

"No secrets," I say with a grin. "Just finding a new normal."

"I think we need beer," Atlas says, getting to his feet.

"Multiple beers," I call after him as he heads into the house.

"It's really good to have you back," Dash says.

THIRTY-ONE

BRIAR

I'm replenishing the beers in the fridge because the guys have made quite a dent in them.

And in the chocolate lasagna.

And the lemon pie.

And the wine—

Okay, so the girls and I may have helped with the last three.

But the guys did their part too.

And based on the laughter that's been growing in frequency and volume over the last few hours, things are going much better than I could have imagined.

I've still been peeking out the window every chance I get, though.

Like now too.

I smile as I see Colt and Dash holding court, their chairs on one side of the fire pit, Royal, Atlas, and Banks on the other.

Colt is saying something that has my brother cackling, Atlas tilting his head back and rolling his eyes up to the sky. Royal's grin is smaller but there. And Banks is laughing full-out, nearly bent in half with it.

Like the old days.

Only in the past I would have been trying to horn in their time together, so ravenous for Colt's attention that I'd play the part of annoying little sister.

Bugging them.

Intruding.

Now, though, I'm content to watch them together. To feel my heart settle, finally settle knowing the worst of the rift has been mended.

It's still going to take time for Colt to find his place, going to take time for everyone to find their way back to, not what we had, but what we'll have now because it's not just the guys and me.

It's the guys and me and Frankie and Maisie. And Aspen and Jade (and their bun in the oven) and Willow *and* Lily.

Our family has grown, changed.

Become so much better than I could have hoped for.

And speaking of family, one member of it loops her arm through mine and draws me away from the window.

"Come on, Peeping Tom," Aspen teases, drawing me into the family room. "We've drawn firm battle lines between the men and women."

"Come and sit by me," Mrs. X says, patting the seat cushion next to her.

I don't argue, just plunk down beside her and give thanks she only came by for dessert, thus avoiding Dash's asshole behavior at dinner.

And the punch he threw.

Because I watched.

Of course I did.

I may have grit my teeth and let the "boys be boys" (this meaning letting them get out their anger and frustration in the most idiotic way possible), but I watched.

Dash didn't hold back with the punch.

And...Colt barely even moved.

I press my thighs together, a ripple of desire flowing through me. Because Colt barely flinched. Because Colt is big and strong and I really like it when he uses all of that big and strong for my benefit. Because Colt may still be healing but he's a *man* through and through and—

"That boy may have the nicest booty on him of all the boys."

I blink, head swiveling toward Mrs. X.

She's clutching her glass of wine and tapping her chin, as though deep in thought about booties and the men they belong to.

Or maybe the women, I think, my lips turning up as I snag my own glass of wine and take a sip.

"Well," Aspen says, "I happen to think that Banks's"—she grins and winks at me—"booty is the best of all the men's booties."

Willow smirks but joins in. "Are you denigrating my man's *booty?*"

Jade rolls her eyes, but I don't miss the slight tinge of pink on her cheeks. "Are we seriously talking about the men's butts?"

"Nope." Mrs. X drinks deeply. "We're talking about booties. Discussing booties of the opposite sex is far less creepy than talking about your young men's butts."

"Is it though?" Willow asks, earning a sharp look from Mrs. X.

"I'll take one thousand for *I'm Glad Frankie is Asleep,* Alex," I say dryly, earning my own sharp look from our adopted grandmother.

"You think I would talk about booties when my sweet little granddaughter is awake?"

"Why do I suddenly have the urge to cover Maisie's ears," Aspen mutters, slowly rocking her sleeping daughter in her arms.

"Because booties may invade her dreams?"

That kind of snark usually comes from Lily (but she's not in town). Or me. Or Willow. Or Aspen.

From Jade, though, especially when paired with a mischievous smile, it has us all freezing in place.

Then Mrs. X grins. "Pregnancy hormones are good for you."
A wink. "For the record, your Royal's booty is also very nice."

Jade rolls her eyes, her cheeks pinkening further, but she doesn't bite.

Aspen does, glancing over at me. "Should we call Lily and loop her in on booty ranking?" Her lips quirk. "Because I will fight to the death on the fact that my man's *booty* is the best booty of them all."

"Them's fighting words," Willow teases.

But Jade surprises us again.

Because she already has her phone out and has dialed Lily.

Something we discover when I hear the tell-tale tone of the video call connecting and turn to see Lily's gorgeous face popping up on the screen.

She holds up her own glass of wine.

"Please tell me that's from Oak Ridge."

Mrs. X pfts. "As if we'd drink anything else now that your man has made it clear he's close with a billionaire winemaker."

Jade passes her phone to Willow so the other woman can more effectively point the video at sweet, gorgeous Maisie. "Jean-Michel also owns the hockey team, the Oakland Eagles, Mrs. X."

She perks up. "He plays hockey?"

"Played," Lily says through the phone. "Apparently, he had an injury and went into the wine business instead." She blows kisses at Maisie, even though the infant has no clue she's there.

But Maisie is irresistible.

And God, I want another baby.

I freeze, that insane thought plastered across a billboard in my mind.

It's far too soon to think about babies. Colt and I are just figuring out our lives together, and Frankie is only now settling in. Plus, my daughter is barely used to sharing the spotlight with Maisie.

A baby would be a disaster.

Thank God Colt and I have been using protection ever since that first night.

"I bet that this Jean-Michel has a nice booty too," Mrs. X says. "Seeing how he played hockey too."

"See!" Aspen cries triumphantly, making Maisie jerk in her hold. "I told you my man has the best *booty* of them all."

There's movement behind her and my lips turn up.

Before I can warn her, Banks leans close.

"You like my *booty*, little spitfire?"

Her cheeks flare pink and she opens her mouth to retort, but Banks just leans a little more forward, kisses her soundly, then tugs Maisie out of her arms. "Less booty talk," he teases, "and more going home to show me *your* booty."

Mrs. X downs her wine, sets the empty glass on the coffee table. "I guess I'm sleeping with my earplugs in tonight."

I still, amusement bubbling up in my chest, but I lose my hold on it when my eyes connect with Lily's on the phone screen.

Then we both start laughing.

And Willow and Jade join in.

The guys, having followed Banks slowly enough to miss all booty talk look at us like we're nuts.

But it doesn't take long for Mrs. X to fill them in and for a debate about booties to commence as they pack up their things and snag the leftovers I set aside for them.

There's no consensus by the time they hit the door and drive away.

I still have my opinion, though.

So maybe that's why when Colt closes and locks the door then turns to face me, I drag my eyes down his body and say,

"You gonna show *me* that booty, honey?"

Thirty-Two

Colt

She never has to ask me twice about getting naked.

I reach for her hand, and we practically race to her bedroom, locking the door behind us. Before I can even think about the condoms in her bathroom or the fact that the blinds are still up, she's pulling at my T-shirt, yanking it over my head.

"Easy, baby," I breathe through a laugh. 'We're not in a rush."

"Speak for yourself." She goes to work on the button and zipper of my jeans.

"Wait—condoms!" I pant, speed walking into her bathroom and digging out the box I stuffed behind some towels on a shelf too high for Frankie to reach.

In the ten seconds it takes me to get back to the bedroom, Briar's naked and waiting on the bed. And I have to take a second to drink her in. She's soft and curvy in all the right places, miles of pale skin ready for my touch.

Sometimes I wonder if my scarred, too-skinny body still turns her on. I need to get back to the gym, put some muscle back on, but—

"What were you thinking about just now?" she asks, holding out a hand to me. "You went from all swoony bad-boy to being deep in thought."

Swoony bad-boy?

I like the sound of that, but it's not the right time for a joke.

"Still having a hard time believing you're mine," I admit instead, kicking off my jeans and sliding onto the bed to stretch out on top of her.

"I've always been yours." Her breath is warm against my face, fingers gentle in my hair. "Scars and all."

Damn, this woman gets me. Always has. Always will.

"What do you need tonight, Briar?"

Curiosity fills those emerald depths. "What do you mean?"

"To date, I've only ever made love to you. So, you've never been fucked."

A smile crosses her pretty features. "Is there is a difference when you're in a relationship?"

"There is. It's subtle, because I love you no matter what we're doing, but there are nuances that are different. I'm sure Lily's told you about Atlas's shenanigans with his whips and—"

"Ew! No, don't do that!" She sticks out her tongue in horror, laughing.

"You girls don't talk?" I'm willing to bet my life she's lying, and by the tell-tale pink in her cheeks, I'm right.

"We do but..."

"Honey, we can talk about everything. Even what our friends are doing, in case there's something you want to try."

She winds her arms around my neck. "Can I tell you a secret?"

"Of course."

"I want to try everything." She pauses. "Okay, not everything. I've watched porn and some stuff is...gross."

"So, no scat play?" I tease.

She makes a gagging sound. "Please tell me you're not into that."

"No. I guess there's a time and place for it, but I don't really have any kinks. You want me to tie you up? Fun. You want me to spank you? Sure thing. Ass play? It's been a long time, so we'll have to explore together. But in general, the only thing I would miss if I didn't have it is oral—both giving and receiving."

"I've never... uh, well, I've never done that."

"No?" I pepper light kisses along her eyelids, tip of her nose, cheeks.

"During our night together, you were all about pleasuring me. I never got the chance to reciprocate."

"Want to try now?"

"Yes." No hesitation.

"Some women think it's degrading but—"

"Fuck that. Just because I haven't done it doesn't mean I don't have opinions. Just watching porn—I find it fascinating. To have that kind of control of your partner's pleasure."

If I ever had any doubt about our compatibility—not that I did—I know now without an iota of doubt that we are.

"On my knees or..." She wiggles out from under me.

"Nah. I mean, we can do that sometime. I like it when you're all dressed up, lipstick on, hair all curly and wild—that's when you can get on your knees. But tonight, let's keep it simple." I flip onto my back and reach down, stroking my cock a few times. He's already wide awake, ready for action.

And Briar is many things, but shy isn't one of them. Not with me anyway. Not the first time we made love, and apparently not tonight.

"What feels good?" she asks.

"Anything you want. Touching me with your fingers is nice. Stroking with both hands. Sucking on my balls is fucking amazing. And kissing the surrounding areas. Just explore, baby. There's literally no way to do it wrong unless you bite me."

"I'll save that for when I'm mad at you," she teases.

"That's fair." I watch as she slides down my body and runs her hand over my crotch.

"And you can't break him," I say lightly. "I mean, technically, you can—but it would take a lot of effort. So don't be afraid to manhandle me. So to speak."

We both chuckle, and I love every second of this.

Not just because she's about to suck my dick—but the intimacy of the moment. Her lack of trepidation in me showing her something new. The way she trusts me so damn completely.

She has beautiful hands with short but well-manicured nails, and she runs them lightly across my groin area. I made sure to do some manscaping after we slept together again the first time, and she seems to appreciate it as she nuzzles the area with her cheek.

Warm fingers close around my cock and a sigh escapes me.

"Fuck, that's nice," I murmur.

"Too soft?" she asks.

"Yeah, but starting out slow and working up to harder is fine."

To my surprise, she lifts my cock and studies it for a moment. She runs a finger along the vein that goes down the center. Then follows the same trail with the tip of her tongue.

Holy Jesus, I'm in heaven.

Watching her is almost as erotic as what she's doing.

Her face disappears as she dips down far enough to cup my balls and suck one into her mouth.

"Just like that, baby." I choke out encouragement.

As much as I want to watch, I want to enjoy it more. Our newfound intimacy is heady, more powerful than any sex I've ever had, and I want to be in this moment with her. Every time we touch it feels like we're adding another brick in the wall of our relationship—building something important and eternal.

I might be a sentimental sap, but four years in a Russian prison can do that to you—I won't even pretend otherwise.

Briar takes her time exploring every inch of my cock, my balls, and the surrounding areas, lavishing attention on my inner thighs, my lower stomach, even my hips. Then she nibbles the head of my cock, and the groan that leaves my chest is long and powerful.

"Fuck, baby, that feels incredible." I reach down, winding my fingers into her soft, silky curls.

When she opens her mouth and swallows half my dick, I hiss from the effort it takes to stay in control.

"Keep that up," I growl, "and I'm not going to last."

I can practically feel her smiling as she wraps one fist around the base and then sucks hard.

"Briar...fuck!" My hips snap up of their own volition.

"I don't know if I can take it all," she murmurs, more to herself than to me.

"Deep throating," I pant, "can be lesson...two... For now, just —oh God!"

I'm fucking her mouth without even realizing I'm doing it, the warm wet cocoon clamping around me just right. And she instinctively sucks harder.

"Baby..." I tighten my grip on her hair, start moving faster, going a little deeper each time. I won't choke her, but this feels too good to stop. "Just a little more—Briar!" The tsunami racing down my spine is unstoppable, and I shoot into her mouth, pulsing over and over.

And she hangs on, swallowing every drop.

My heart is hammering against my ribs, skin flushed with pleasure, and all I can do is lie there—staring at the ceiling as I try to find my breath.

She sits up, wiping her mouth with the back of her hand. "Yum."

My eyes snap to hers. "Yeah? You like a little salt with your hot dog?"

Laughter bubbles out of her. "As a matter of fact, I do." Then the laughter fades, replaced with a look of uncertainty. "Was it... okay?"

"Okay?" I shake my head. "No. It was not okay—it was fucking phenomenal. Get up here." I reach out and pull her against me, taking her lips greedily. I can taste the remnants of my semen on her tongue and when it's part of kissing her, it's amazing.

Everything with Briar is amazing.

"So...does that count as fucking or making love?" she asks when she lifts her head.

"That counts as the love of my life doing beautifully dirty things to her man. Like I said, it's more nuanced than that when you're in a committed, loving relationship. But trust me—when I truly fuck you—you'll know."

She cocks her head. "Can that be...now?"

"Oh, yeah."

THIRTY-THREE

BRIAR

"And then we add..."

Colt glances down at my recipe—and seriously, thank God I laminated it because it's covered with flour and egg goo and who knows what else.

I can just wipe it clean later.

Instead of having to rewrite the whole thing.

Maybe I need to laminate everything in the house for easy cleanup.

Grinning, I watch my man and my daughter lean close as they scrutinize the paper.

"...three-quarters of a cup of heavy whipping cream."

"That's this one, Daddy!" Frankie says, reaching for the carton and holding it up.

Colt's smile for her—

God, it's so beautiful it's almost painful, piercing my heart somewhere deep inside and burying itself there, never to be shaken free.

Because I've felt that same thing for Frankie, for the beauty we created together.

So, seeing the clear evidence of his love for her...

Yeah, it may be the most beautiful thing I've ever had the privilege to witness.

So much so, I don't jump in to help them, don't clean up the mess they're creating—on the recipe card and the counters *and* the floor. I don't chime in that they're mixing too vigorously or that the pie crusts are overfull.

I just lean back against the opposite counter and soak in seeing the man I love creating a memory with our daughter.

He's missed so much.

Yet, he's here right now, creating this moment in time.

And Frankie, because of all the love and time her uncles have given her over the last four (and three-quarters) years, time and love I'm so damned thankful for because it made her the girl she is today—confident in that love, comfortable in her place in the world, knowing that she's safe and protected and valued for who she is—soaks it all in.

And flourishes even more.

Because even though Colt missed so much, he's here now.

He's engaged.

He listens and puts the time in.

It also doesn't hurt that he's tall enough to reach the oven and strong enough to slide the cookie sheet with those overfull pies in.

I'll have a mess to clean up later, that's for sure.

But it's a mess I'll clean up with a smile—

And with my daughter and my man scrubbing dishes beside me.

First, though, we're going to have pie.

———

"Can we get this one, Mom?" Frankie asks, jumping up and down and pointing to a truly ginormous Christmas tree. "Can we?!"

"I'm not sure it will fit on top of the car, sweetie," I say, eyeing the size of the trunk and mentally calculating how long it will take to hack through it with the dull bow saw the kid at the front handed us when we entered the tree lot.

Spoiler alert, it will take approximately one million years.

Hyperbole? Maybe.

A giant tree filled with a shit-ton of needles I want to sweep up over the next weeks (and months)? God, no.

"It'll fit," Colt says, immediately crouching down and eying the trunk.

"Well, I don't think that you'll want to saw through it," I try. "That'll take forever, right?" I ask, lifting my brows pointedly.

A point he misses because he turns to Frankie. "This the one you want, sweetheart?"

She nods.

He looks at me. "You approve, baby?"

"It's a beautiful tree, honey," I say, and it's not a lie. My daughter picked out a truly gorgeous Douglas fir, even and straight, no holes. If it wasn't gigantic, I'd be all over it. "But—"

He lays down, shoving the branches out of the way.

"Colt."

His eyes come to mine. "We don't need—"

"You like the tree. Frankie likes the tree." He positions the saw. "My girls are getting what they want."

Then he starts sawing.

And I find that I suddenly have to unzip my hoodie.

Thanks, SoCal heat.

Except it's not just the fact that it's December and nearly eighty degrees...it's also the fact that Colt is sawing and I'm watching the muscles on his forearms, along with his biceps and triceps flex as he cuts through the trunk.

Then there's the fact that his shirt has ridden up a couple of inches, exposing those dips near his hips that I ran my tongue over only the night before.

And also maybe his words.

My girls are getting what they want.

Sigh.

I really, really love my man.

"Are you going to help Daddy cut down our super-duper big tree, Mommy?" Frankie asks, skipping around the branches.

"No," Atlas says, bumping his shoulder against mine as he and Royal walk by, his voice dropping when he adds for my ears only, "she's too busy drooling."

I swat at his chest.

"He's not lying." Royal smirks. "Pull it together, Thorny."

I swat at him too, but he just grins and loops an arm around Jade as she studies a nearby tree—though it's not nearly as big as ours—pulling her back against his chest.

Banks is already lugging his tree to the road, Aspen, who's holding Maisie (adorably decked out in a Christmas-themed outfit) trailing him.

And Willow's supervising Dash as he ties their tree to the roof of their SUV.

Lily's on tour, but I don't miss that Atlas has finished teasing me and started getting serious about cutting down a nearby pine.

Everyone's paired up.

Domesticated.

I smile.

Because this year, Christmas spirit is all around us.

And truly, life can't get any better.

———

"What if he says my list is too long?" Frankie asks, her fingers laced with mine, gently swinging our hands back and forth, back and forth.

I glance ahead of us at the line to see Santa, see that it's showing no sign of moving.

So, I crouch down in front of my daughter and gently grasp her shoulders.

"You know that the real magic of Santa is not that he gives you everything you want, but what you need, baby."

"But you said we need to go shopping for underwear after this. What if he knows that's what I need, and he doesn't get me anything on my list?"

My lips twitch.

Because fuck my daughter is the best.

She never fails to leave me smiling.

"Sometimes Santa brings underwear," I tell her because that's the reality of the world we live in, and lots of kids aren't as privileged as my girl is (who's getting the number one item on the list she's holding so tightly—a Polly Panda doll—because I preordered it a month ago when it looked like it was going to be this Christmas's hottest item for four and three-quarters-year-olds). "But oftentimes Santa does his best to make it both something you want *and* something you need."

She considers that for a long moment.

Then nods.

I straighten and we close the gap that's opened up between us and the next family in line, and she's reviewing her carefully written list as Colt comes back with the coffees he left to snag for us.

Because our girl needed to get to Santa first thing this morning.

And she certainly didn't care that he and I had been up late last night—*very* late—going through our own list.

And one that's entirely filled with things that bring us both pleasure.

"All good?" he asks as we sip and keep shuffling forward.

"Frankie's in deep introspection about her list for Santa."

"Why's that?"

Frankie doesn't even look up from the paper she's perusing. "Because I don't want Santa to bring me underwear."

Colt's mouth drops open.

I stifle my laughter as I lift on tiptoe and murmur in his ear, "I'll explain later."

"I'm not sure I want to know." He tugs a lock of my hair.

"You do," I say. "Because it's about our daughter."

His face goes soft. "Yeah, baby," he says. "You're right. I want to know."

"I love you," I whisper.

"I love you too," he whispers back.

"Santa," I hear Frankie say. "I've been a very good girl this year so can you not bring me underwear?"

Colt looks at me.

I look at him.

Then we both start laughing.

And I do it thinking that life can't get any better.

———

The next week, exhausted after a long—and messy—night of helping Frankie decorate cookies for her preschool teachers and aides (which means there were a *lot* of cookies to decorate), Colt almost immediately falls asleep next to me.

I get it, Frankie's a lot. This time of year is a lot.

And he's been killing himself to do it all...and to do it all big.

Hitting the gym to get his strength back.

Learning the ropes from Dash to see if he wants to buy into Dash's security company.

Volunteering at the school gingerbread house decorating event.

Decorating our ginormous tree with a truly absurd amount of lights and ornaments and tinsel.

Spending hours shopping for Christmas presents and then wrapping them carefully and arranging them under the tree.

I've tried to remind him that he has time, that he doesn't have to cram it all in at once.

But...

It's Christmas. His first Christmas with us as a family, with him as a father, with him as a member of a growing family.

So yeah, he's putting in the time.

And I love him for it.

He just...needs to chill.

I'll remind him of that tomorrow. Tonight, I'm going to enjoy the fact that Frankie's as tuckered out as him and read my book.

So I do exactly that.

Staying up far too late, but fully stuck in that just-one-more-chapter mode, it's not until well after midnight that I put my Kindle aside and start to turn off the light—

"No!"

I jerk, eyes flying to Colt. He's asleep, his brows pulled tightly together. "Honey?" I ask quietly.

"No!" he says again, this time paired with a flinch, his big body thrashing on the bed. "Don't!"

He's having a nightmare.

I reach over, settle my hand on his arm, and—

Gasp as I'm suddenly on my back, my arm twisted above my head, his fingers wrapped so tightly around my wrist pain ripples up my arm.

"Colt," I say. "It's me, baby. It's—"

His eyes are open but unfocused and his grip tightens.

Going so tight I whimper in pain.

He stills.

Then he's releasing me, horror rippling across his face. "Fuck, Briar," he says immediately rolling off me. "Fuck, I'm so sorry." He sits up, hands going to either side of his head, gripping his hair so tightly I worry he might pull it out by the roots. Then he turns his gaze back to mine. "I'm so sorry. I didn't mean to. You have to believe me. You—"

I sit up, shifting so I'm sitting behind him. He hesitates then reaches out for my hand, carefully lifting it and pressing his lips to the reddened marks on my wrist.

"It's okay," I say. "I'm okay."

"I hurt you."

"Colt," I say. "Stop. You were having a nightmare. It's okay. We'll be okay."

He shakes his head.

"But we do need to talk about it, honey." Because he's been having too many of them. Because this one was worse than the rest. Because he won't be able to sleep beside me if he's worried he's going to hurt me. "And we need to find a way to make them stop."

He exhales. "I should be over this shit. I'm home safe. I have everything I ever dreamed of."

"And that makes it even scarier." I slide his fingers through mine. "Knowing how good it can be, knowing how precious it is. Knowing what living without it is like."

His throat works before he whispers on a rasp, "Yeah."

"Do you love me?"

His eyes lock onto mine. "God, yes, Briar."

"And do you love Frankie?"

Those blue eyes cloud. "Of course, I do. How could you think—"

"I don't think anything except that *because* of that, you can't bury what happened to you."

His inhale is sharp.

"You need to be your best self for me and Frankie." A beat. "And for yourself."

He nods but his expression is agonized. "I know. I just...I've always handled this shit on my own or with Dash."

"Then start by talking to him, honey."

"I don't know if he's ready for that."

I squeeze his fingers. "Honestly, I think he needs you to need *him*. I think after all that's happened that will heal him in a way you can't even imagine." I draw him back down into bed beside me. "But I get if that's too much for you after all this time. So, if it's not Dash, we need to find you someone else you can talk to."

I wrap my arms around him, hold him tight.

He's still, stiff. Hurting and scared and haunted by nightmares.

But he's also Colt.

The man I love, the one who will do anything for Frankie and me.

His body softens and he hugs me back, lips coming to my ear.

"I'll talk to Dash in the morning."

Thirty-Four

Colt

Engagement rings are expensive. I don't give a shit about the money, but I didn't realize I could buy a house—somewhere other than Los Angeles—for the money I'm about to drop on Briar's ring. Atlas is haggling with the jeweler, someone he uses exclusively, and they seem to enjoy the back and forth.

The prices are making my head spin, but I want Briar to have the most beautiful ring imaginable. In fact, I want her and Frankie to have everything I can possibly provide, which is why I'm considering becoming a partner in Dash's security business. He protested when I told him I wanted to give him cash for half the value of the company, and we did a bit of haggling too. Next week, we're going to see a financial planner that Atlas recommended to sort out the details.

Deep down, I think it will be good for us. He feels like he's helping me, even though I've had more private security job offers in the last two weeks than most people have in their entire lives. Word got out through the marine grapevine, and my phone hasn't stopped buzzing.

Working with Dash feels like the right move, though.

He's family.

The brother I chose and soon he'll be my brother-in-law legally too.

Things are finally falling into place, both personally and professionally.

My body is still healing, but I'm a lot better and I've started gaining stamina and rebuilding the muscle I lost in that Russian hell hole. That's another thing that Dash and I have been sharing lately. As usual, Briar was right; he just needed to feel needed. Now that he does, we're back on an even keel.

It won't always be like this, but short-term, it's turned out to be a good thing for both of us.

I'm also seeing a therapist.

I was resistant at first—tough guys don't go to therapy—but Briar's words resonated in a way that nothing else had.

"You need to be your best self for me and Frankie."

Yeah, I absolutely do, and if therapy is one of the ways I get there, I'm all in.

I finally asked Dash, who got a name from Royal, who got it from Atlas. Only one appointment so far but I like her. Turns out she's an Air Force veteran with some trauma of her own, making it a lot easier for me to open up. She said everything I'm going through—the nightmares, occasional anxiety, frustration with my physical injuries—is all normal. She also expressed that she thinks I'm doing great, all things considered.

Which is a relief because I don't want to be a burden on Briar or Frankie. Frankie needs her dad and there's nothing I won't do to make sure I'm the father she both needs and wants. It still hits me right in the feels every time she calls me Daddy.

"You're sure you want the platinum?" the jeweler is asking me.

I snap back to the present and nod. "Yes. Everything she owns is either platinum or silver. She says gold doesn't go well with her skin."

The jeweler nods and presents me with an invoice.

I pull out my brand new platinum American Express card and hand it to him.

"This is a big step," Atlas says to me.

"It's time. Past time for Briar and me."

He shakes his head. "Look at this—the five of us essentially all wifed up. How the fuck did this happen?"

"We met some very special women."

"That we did." He's thoughtful. "You know, I have to tell you something... Originally, the idea of you and Briar together kind of grossed me out. But now..."

"Now?" I'm curious about his thought process since I know he's come to terms with everything.

"Now it feels right—I don't know that there's anyone *else* that I would truly trust with her. Anyone else I would be a thousand percent confident would never hurt her, physically or otherwise."

"Never gonna happen," I growl.

"I know. That's why it's right."

"I tried not to love her," I admit. "But the harder I tried not to love her the stronger the feelings got, until I couldn't ignore them anymore."

"If things had gone down differently in Russia, what was your plan with regard to her?"

"I was going to talk to Dash the minute I got back."

"He would've been pissed off back then too."

We chuckle, because he's right.

Thankfully, that nonsense is over now. Dash and I are spending a lot of time together again. Just like the old days. It's a relief for Briar too because it stressed her out when we were at odds.

The jeweler disappears into the back to package up the ring just as Atlas's phone rings.

"It's Briar," he says, grimacing.

"Go ahead and take it. We don't want her to get suspicious.

We're done here anyway. I'll be out as soon as he finishes up whatever he's doing."

"Okay." He puts the phone to his ear. "Hey, what's up?"

I fidget while the jeweler runs my card and finally comes out with the ring nestled in an ornate gift bag.

"Thank you," I say.

"It was a pleasure doing business with you, Mr. Blackwood."

"Likewise."

I've been dreaming about marrying Briar for years and I've just taken a major step toward making that happen. And I can't wait to propose.

Atlas has been throwing ideas at me—all completely ridiculous and over-the-top—so I'm trying to come up with a plan that falls somewhere between asking her while I'm deep inside her and renting out the top of the Eiffel Tower.

It has to be something romantic but private, because I know she'll want it to be just us. I've tossed around the idea of asking Frankie but decided Briar needs the whole romantic gesture first. *Then* we can talk to Frankie. As much as I love my kid, a four-and-three-quarters-year-old is not telling me whether or not I can marry her mom.

I walk outside and my step falters.

Atlas is standing next to his Bentley, hands on his hips. There's a nondescript black sedan parked next to him, a man in sunglasses standing beside it, and Atlas does not look at all amused.

Oh, hell.

I recognize the guy right away.

My handler.

What. The. Fuck.

I stride in their direction with a scowl.

"What are you doing here, Forrester?" I demand.

"You know this douche waffle?" Atlas asks, peering at me over the top of his sunglasses.

"I do." I turn back to Nathan Forrester. "So? What's going on? I told you I'm out."

"I know." He holds up his hands in a placating gesture. "But this is different."

"It's not. I'm done. I don't want anything to do with—"

"Colt, it's *Igor*."

This time I freeze, my gaze snapping to his.

"What?"

He holds out his phone. "This came in this morning through back channels."

The picture on the screen makes my blood run cold.

Igor, my old teammate and the man who got me out of Siberian hell, is in chains, hanging from the ceiling of what looks like an old warehouse. His face is beaten beyond recognition, but I recognize the tattoo of an eagle on his right shoulder and biceps —it's the mascot from our college hockey team. So, it's definitely him.

There are bloody wounds all over his torso, his feet are bare and dirty, and there's a pool of blood below him.

No one has to tell me it's bad.

Or that he's going to die if someone doesn't stage a rescue operation.

"Do we know where he is?" I ask, my training kicking in automatically. "Where did the intel come from?"

"We have an idea." Forrester gives me a quick rundown.

"I need an hour or two," I say.

"Colt." Atlas's voice is low, tight, but he saw the picture. He has to understand.

"I *know*," I say without looking at him. "But I wouldn't be here if not for Igor."

"Call me when you're ready for me to pick you up," Forrester says. "We have a plane waiting to take us to D.C. And you can pick your team."

I don't even hesitate because I'm going off the books with this one. "Landon Grimshaw and Elliott Rageis."

Forrester is one of those suit types who never smiles. He literally epitomizes everything stereotypical about spy organizations. But when I mention Grim and Rage, he almost smiles. Almost.

"I need to get home," I tell Atlas.

He grimaces. "What are you going to tell Briar?"

"I'll figure it out."

Yeah, and it's not going to be good enough.

Briar and Frankie are my priorities, but this is a debt of honor —it's not optional.

Igor risked his life to get me out of Russia.

If not for him, I wouldn't have Briar and Frankie.

One last mission, I tell myself blandly. *Please forgive me, baby.*

THIRTY-FIVE

BRIAR

"What the fuck?" I whisper, mind spinning, stomach churning.

Terror wars with...happiness.

And more terror.

But mostly...happiness.

Such pure, unfettered happiness that I snag my phone from the counter, jabbing at the screen and hitting a number.

"Hey, what's up?" Atlas asks.

I exhale, try to keep my tone neutral. "Can you cover the Conrad meeting this afternoon?"

A pause. "Yes. Is everything okay?"

"Yes, I just...need to get home so I can take care of something with Frankie."

There's another pause. "I'm not sure I believe that."

"I—"

"But I know that I'll probably hear about it soon enough, so don't bother making up another lie." He chuckles. "Do what you need to do, Briar. I'll take care of Conrad."

"Thanks, I appreciate it."

There's another voice in the background, and Atlas's voice turns irritated.

"Is everything—?"

"I've gotta go, Briar."

"I—"

"Talk to you later."

He hangs up.

I contemplate that weirdness for a moment. Then my eyes go back to the counter. I'll worry about my changeable and grumpy-far-too-often boss later.

Right now, I have to get home.

And tell Colt.

I snag the positive pregnancy tests—yup, that's tests plural, and yes that's pregnant as in *pregnant* because apparently Colt has super sperm or I have super eggs or together our bodies just get super freaking pregnant because we made Frankie that weekend and—

I settle my hand on my belly.

We made this baby.

And he's going to be here every step of the way.

I grin, shove the tests into my purse, and hurry down to my car.

Colt dropped Frankie off at school this morning then had some errands to run afterward. Ever since he bought a car, he's been slowly filling out his days without me. I miss all the one-on-one time but know he needs to get on with rebuilding his life, especially since my days are filled with work and our family. Which means it's not unlikely that he'll be hanging with Dash or Banks, but even if he's not home when I get there, I know he won't be far behind me because he promised Frankie he'd pick her up from school.

So, if he's there, we'll celebrate without a four-and-three-quarters-year-old.

If he's *not* there, I'll cook something special and we'll celebrate tonight with good food.

Like peanut butter and pickles.

Oy.

Pregnancy cravings.

Good food will be something that's *not* peanut butter and pickles.

Maybe a salad and chicken breasts—

My stomach churns.

Right, enough about food.

If Colt's not home, I've got my next steps.

SoCal traffic isn't all that kind but since it's not rush hour, it doesn't take too long to get back to the house.

And my heart leaps when I see Colt's SUV in the garage.

He's home.

Eek!

I park, snag my purse, and bustle into the house. "Colt!" I call as I rush through the kitchen. "I need to talk…"

But my words trail off when I see he's wearing his camouflage pants and a tight beige long-sleeved shirt—the same uniform I've seen him wear dozens of times, if not more. The same clothes he wore when…he shipped off last time.

And holding his beat up duffle bag in one hand.

He sets it on the ground as I skid to a halt. "Baby," he murmurs.

I know what he's going to say.

I see it on his face.

I feel it pierce my heart.

And I still ask "What's happening?" anyway.

He takes a step toward me, and I skitter back a pace. He freezes.

"What's happening, Colt?"

"Baby," he says a second time, even more gently. "I have to go."

I close my eyes. "You promised," I whisper.

And he's suddenly there, hands on my shoulders, face close to mine when I peel back my lids. "It's Igor, he's in trouble."

I don't want Colt's friend and savior to be in trouble, don't want him to get hurt. But—

Pain ripples through me.

Because he *promised* he would stay.

Because this is history repeating itself.

Because I'm going to be alone and—

A sob bubbles up in my chest but I force it down, grasp on to the tendrils of anger.

It feels so much better to be angry.

Instead of hurt.

I lift my chin. "You can't go."

His voice is beyond gentle. "I have to, baby. I owe him my life." He cups my jaw. "I wouldn't be here if it wasn't for him."

This is...

My worst nightmare.

No, it's worse than my worst nightmare because this time Frankie is going to be hurt too.

"I need you to find another way to help Igor," I order. "Because you can't leave. Not when you promised me, not when you promised *Frankie* you'd stay."

Remorse ripples across his face but I know it's not going to change anything, least of all his mind about this—I can see that in the lines of his expression, feel it in the gentle way he trails his fingers across my cheek, slides them down to cup my jaw. "They're hurting him, baby. I need to go help get him out."

That gets me.

I'm not a monster.

I don't want one of Colt's friends to be in danger.

So, I suck in a breath, hold it tightly, and do my best to be rational about this. "I'll worry," I whisper. "I'll worry but I'll keep it together, will explain it all to Frankie—"

His body starts to relax.

"*If* you tell me that no one else can do this—"

He goes stiff.

"*If* you tell me that no one else can go in and get him out but you, you'll have my blessing."

He clenches his jaw.

And I see the truth in his beautiful sapphire eyes.

There are other people who could do this rescue mission.

Other people he could call on to save his friend when he's still recovering from being tortured, when he's not at full strength, when he's still suffering from flashbacks, when...

Going means having to leave Frankie and me and—my fingers clench on the strap of my purse, the pregnancy tests rattling inside like fate's worst joke—our baby.

He's going to make a deliberate choice to leave all three of us.

After he promised—*promised*—to stay.

"If you leave us again," I rasp, the words torn out of me, "you can't come back. I won't give you a third chance to hurt us."

"Baby," he says, gently pulling me against his chest and wrapping his arms around me. "I'll be back before you know it. And then I will never leave you again. I promise."

More promises.

Promises he'll break.

I pull out of his hold.

"I love you," he murmurs, cupping my face in both of his hands. "I'm coming back, but I have to do this."

Words.

Words that don't matter, not when he's leaving again.

That don't matter when he drops his hands away, picks up his duffle, and heads out to the garage, the door clicking softly closed behind him.

The sob escapes, and I lose my battle against my tears, feeling them sliding down my cheeks, dripping off my jaw, soaking into the collar of my shirt.

I sink to the floor, purse hitting it beside me, contents scattering, the tests—oh God, the tests—bringing nothing but pain now. Pain and heartbreak and the reminder that I'm not enough and I won't ever be.

That thought ricochets through me so violently, that when I glance down, I expect there to be a gaping hole in my chest where my heart used to be.

But it's whole.

I'm whole.

On the outside.

And I need to pull it together so that Frankie never thinks that she's not enough.

Never looks at herself in the mirror and wonders why her father wouldn't stick around.

And I'll make sure this new baby doesn't think that either.

I wipe my tears, move to the stairs. I'll splash some water on my face, fix my makeup, and I'll get myself together so I can get my daughter from school and she doesn't know that I've been broken into a thousand pieces.

That I've lost something that won't ever come back.

Only when I get there, I find my knees buckling again, the tears coming fast and furious.

Because on the edge of the bed...is a bundle of letters.

THIRTY-SIX

COLT

Flying into one of the armpits of hell means a long, uncomfortable ride on a military cargo plane. It's loud, cold, and...unyielding.

My thoughts are unyielding as well.

I broke my promise to the two girls I love most in the world.

Hell, I broke my promise to myself.

When I was in Siberia, I promised myself, fate, and all the gods in every religion that if I got out of there—if I got another chance to be with Briar—I would never leave her again. That my need for her far outweighs my need to right the wrongs in the world.

Yet here I am.

On this fucking plane heading to a remote outstation in the wilderness of Finland, where we can hike to where we believe they're holding Igor. If we're wrong, and there's a trap waiting for us, we're all dead. If we're right and they outgun us, we're all dead. If we're wrong and there's no one there, I'm going to wish I was dead because I know Igor can't last much longer.

"You okay?" Landon "Grim" Grimshaw studies my face carefully.

We served together when I was first deployed. He was my commanding officer then, a big, stand-up guy with a moral code that matches my own and fighting skills like no one I've ever seen. Not even me. When people joke about being able to kill someone twenty-seven ways with one hand tied behind their back? That's Grim.

He's six feet four inches of solid muscle, with a short, scruffy beard and piercing dark eyes. Men give him a wide berth, women swarm to him like bees to honey, and bad guys are terrified.

He's out of the military, working private security for a firm in Vegas, but if anyone could help me get Igor out, it's Grim.

And just like Dash has always been my sidekick, Elliott "Rage" Rageis is his. I don't know exactly how long they've been friends but even though I'd never met him until today, Grim talked about him enough to make me feel like we're already friends. Kind of the way I talked about my brothers.

Rage doesn't truly know me either, but he came because Grim asked. So, I have mad respect for him. I'm also aware of his martial arts training. He's not a killer so much as a fighter. I watched a video of an MMA fight where he fought and he's beautiful to watch.

And now the three of us, along with a small group of Navy SEALs, are going in to get Igor.

"Colt?" Grim is still staring at me. "You are definitely not in a good head space. What's going on?"

"Sorry. I left things a mess back home."

"How come?"

"I finally got my girl back, found out we had a kid while I was in training, and just bought a ring. I promised her I was done."

"She understands this is a one-off, doesn't she?"

"I don't..." I shake my head. "She does but I promised her I'd never leave her and Frankie again. And yet, I just did."

There's a strange, momentary haunted look in Grim's eyes, as if he's experienced something similar. Then it's gone, and he shrugs. "If there's something more important than this mission, why are you here?"

"I owe him my life. If he hadn't risked his to get me out of that prison, I'd be dead and I wouldn't have gotten back to my girl and my kid."

"That's fair, but you have to get your head in the game or you're no good to any of us. Igor needs you focused, and so do the rest of us. You're the team leader here, Colt. You have to lead."

"I will!" I snap. Then I close my eyes and take a breath. "Sorry. But I've got this. I just—the look in her eyes when I left. She said she wouldn't give me a third chance. And if I ruined things with us over this, I don't know what I'll do."

"You'll figure it out. Lots of people co-parent without being together."

"You don't understand."

"Then tell me."

"She's my life—my family. Her and Frankie and the boys."

"You're talking about Dash and the guys you went to college with."

"Yeah. And that includes Igor. I mean, he wasn't as close to us as the others—he barely spoke English then, or at least, he pretended not to. But I recognized a fellow soldier, so I knew there was more to him than met the eye. Now I owe him my life."

"You don't," he says quietly, waiting until I meet his gaze to continue. "He didn't rescue you in Siberia because he expected some kind of debt of honor. He rescued you because it was the right thing to do and he was in a position to do so. Maybe you're not in that position this time."

"I am," I say firmly. "Because if I don't, and he dies, I'll never forgive myself."

"You can win your girl back if we get Igor out. You can't replace him if we don't."

I nod.

"So, if you want to do that, without getting yourself killed, you need to be all in. This job can't be done with one foot out the door. You listening to me, marine?"

It's been a long time since anyone called me that.

"Yes, sir." I momentarily fall back into the command structure.

But he's reminded me that I will get myself—and the rest of the team—killed if I don't focus.

I'm sorry, baby.

I'll be home soon.

I promise.

"Let's do this," I say quietly.

————

Igor's body is limp, lifeless, as we load him onto the plane a day later.

But he's alive.

Barely.

And it's going to take a lot of medical attention to help him but he's alive.

Fuck.

I don't know how anyone could take so much and still survive, but Igor's one of the toughest men I've ever known. Both on and off the ice. As tough as Grim, as deadly as Rage, as sneaky and stealthy as me. He's the whole damn package.

He mumbles groggily. It's in Russian but I get the gist of it.

"You're a crazy motherfucker."

"Oh, because you were completely sane when you got me out of Siberia?"

"At least you could walk." His voice is thready, like it's taking a lot out of him to talk.

"Just rest, buddy. We'll be at Ramstein in a few hours, and you'll get help." We're not too far from the air base in Germany.

"There better be pretty nurses." He says that in English and all of us chuckle.

"I'll try to arrange that."

One of the SEALs is a medic, so Igor has an IV of antibiotics going, while we try to get him to drink a little water. He smells vile, and I've never seen anyone quite so filthy, but he gets a pass. Hopefully, there will be a pretty nurse to give him a sponge bath or five. He deserves that much.

Now that it's over, I try not to dwell on how close it was.

How they were in the process of moving him, which made it easy to free him but a lot more dangerous.

How they were somehow expecting us and if not for the skills of the SEALs this could have gone very, very wrong.

How doing the right thing was somehow tempered by the danger. By the knowledge that I have someone—multiple people —to go home to, so the risk is no longer worth the reward.

They chose the guy with no family to speak of—at least, not from where they were sitting.

Four guys I went to college with and the sister of one of them don't count as a "family." Not to alphabet soup government agencies. But to me, they're everything. Worth everything. And my last debt is paid. There's nothing else for me to prove.

I'm going home to my family—and I will beg and grovel until Briar forgives me.

I have pictures of Igor, in case she needs a little nudge in the direction of compassion, because she has that in spades. She'll be mad for a while, but it's only been six days. I can't believe she'd write me off that quickly.

"You've got that same pensive scowl on your face you had on the way to Finland," Grim says, kicking my boot.

I chuckle, shaking my head at him.

He took the biggest hit on the team, going toe to toe with the man in charge. They went over the side of a cliff, rolling and tumbling down hundreds of feet, kicking and fighting. The other douchebag broke his neck. Grim wound up with a few broken ribs—but he still helped carry Igor through the woods and to the plane. Still fought off the last two guys who followed us, with a little help from Rage, who ended them with two spectacularly aimed head shots from a gun in each hand.

The exhilaration and adrenaline rush that comes from the danger and excitement is still there, but it's no longer something I crave. It was there and gone before I had time to enjoy it. Because Igor could still die. Because I don't know if Briar is going to forgive me.

It wasn't even a full week.

"Your girl's going to be pissed, huh?"

"Yeah, but I already bought the ring. She's going to say yes."

"The ladies always do fall for your charm," he says wryly.

"It's a gift." I pause. "What about you? You have anyone back home?"

"No time for that," he grumbles. "My sister has a kid, so I'll go stay with her while these ribs heal, help with the baby, have a little family time."

"I'm sure she's great, but what about your own needs?"

"Sex is easy."

"That's not what I'm talking about, dickhead."

"Grim doesn't believe in love," Rage says, rolling his eyes.

"Oh, and you do?" Grim asks him.

Rage shrugs. "Under the right circumstances, sure. I just haven't met her yet. When I do, I'll be ready."

"When you meet the right one, you just know," I tell Grim. "Trust me on this. You think that's some romantic nonsense but it's true. I always knew with Briar, but she was initially too young. Then there was the whole issue of her brother losing his mind at the idea of his sister falling in love. It was always there, though."

Grim shudders slightly. "Fuck that. Relationships are way too much of a distraction."

Rage and I laugh.

"It's not like you're dating anyone for more than a night or two at a time," Grim says to Rage.

They go back and forth for a while, but I just close my eyes, letting my thoughts drift away. Drift...home.

It's Saturday, so I probably won't get home until tomorrow since we have to stop in Germany first. But then I'll either catch a military flight heading west or get on a commercial plane because no matter what I have to do, I'm going to be there for Sunday dinner.

THIRTY-SEVEN

BRIAR

I'm in bed, trying to sleep, hating how empty it feels.

Hating this entire week and how empty my life feels.

Making excuses to Frankie and pretending to be sick so I can work from home, thus avoiding Atlas and his far too keen sense of knowing when something's wrong. Putting off a planned shopping expedition with Willow and Aspen for baby clothes for Jade.

Because I can barely keep it together knowing that history is repeating itself, but I know I don't have a snowball's chance in hell doing it while surrounded by adorable baby clothes.

I sigh and roll to my side, closing my eyes and trying to tamp down on the misery.

Instead, it just grows because I think about the lie I told to explain his absence—Colt needing to go to D.C. for a debrief.

I don't like lying to my family and I already kept too much from them over the years about Colt and Frankie and me, but we might not find a way forward together after this and I won't do anything to harm his relationships.

I sigh again, flop over to my other side.

Lies. Broken promises. Heartbreak. And...worry.

I've been worrying myself into that sick.

Worrying he'll get hurt.

Worrying he won't make it back alive.

Worrying his friend will die and him leaving will be for naught.

Worrying what I'll tell the guys and Frankie if he *doesn't* come back.

"Enough," I hiss, rolling to my back and staring up at the dark ceiling. Sleep isn't going to come. I should just grab my laptop, get up, and do something productive instead of continuing to chastise myself.

I push up, flick on the light, and don't reach for my laptop.

Productive isn't going to happen.

Instead, I open the drawer and reach for the TV remote.

Only, instead of my fingers closing around the remote, they bump into a bundle of papers.

No.

A bundle of *letters.*

Colt's letters.

So many of them, he wrote to me.

And I haven't been able to bring myself to open them, to read them.

Because he left.

Because it hurts too much.

Because I need to slam the steel door on those thoughts in my mind—if I don't, I won't be able to function—

Like I've been functioning so well?

Existing like a half zombie.

Hiding from my family.

So here in the quiet darkness of night, I rip off the Band-Aid.

I pull out the bundle.

And I open the first letter.

...God, Briar. I've never felt like this before. As

though I've left half of myself behind. Honestly, it's fucking with my head, baby. The only time I can keep things together is when I write to you, but since being a soldier is the only thing I know how to be, I have to suck it up and ignore the fact that I feel like a lovesick puppy and focus.

I miss you, baby.

-C

P.S. Be prepared to get a lot more letters...since it's the only time I can get my shit together and all.

I laugh and it's watery.

That's so Colt...and it's sad. We've talked about his future, about him finding his place in the family, about figuring out his next steps. But did he—or more concernedly—*does* he think that all he is, is a soldier?

Because he needs to know that he's so much more than just a soldier.

He needs to know—

A sob bubbles up in my chest.

Then I open the next letter.

...I dreamed about you last night. It was so real that I could have sworn you were right here next to me when I woke up. Then I realized I was in the twin bed with the shitty mattress and government issued blankets and my single pathetic pillow (they really don't want us getting soft with brick-like pillows and scratchy blankets)...and fuck, baby, I so wanted to be home. To be beside you.

I can't wait to dream about you again tonight, baby.

-C

He dreamed about me. He thought about me so much he had trouble focusing.

He wanted to be home.

...today was a fucked-up day. One of the guys I've been training with got careless. And then things got bad. Seriously fucking bad. We're lucky no one died, in all honesty, and now I'm left wondering why I'm doing this. I could be home with you and the guys, building the life we planned together that weekend. I just...if I was home what would I be doing? Like really doing? What difference would I be making? At least if I'm here, I know we're doing real work that is going to make a difference. It's direct. It's hands on. It's...fuck, but it's all I know how to do. And I need to do something to prove to the guys, to you, to Dash that I'm worthy of being in their lives. In your life, baby.

I promise you that I'll prove it.

I promise you that I'll be home as soon as I can.

-C

He needs to prove that he's worthy?
Does he still think that?
My lungs hitch, and tears start sliding down my cheeks.
And I can't stop.
I tear open letter after letter.

...training was really shitty today, but I made it through, so I'm a step closer to ready for my first mission. I'm so fucking exhausted, though, that I'm thinking about nothing except your smile. And how once the mission's done, I'll finally get to see it somewhere that's not just my dreams...

...I dreamed about you last night again. About the way you got so mad at Dash for sneaking the cookies you were baking. I have a confession. I stole them too...

...I think I'm going insane. I swore I caught a hint of your perfume today. I ended up following the agent who was wearing it and she sprayed some on a piece of paper for me. I sniffed it like an addict. And now it's tucked under my pillow...

...I'm getting ready to fly out, baby. So, this may be my last letter for a while. But know that I'll be thinking about you every spare second and I'll be dreaming about you every night. I'm going to make this go as quickly as possible so I can get home to you...

And that's the last one.

The last letter.

Some many of them, so many thoughts about me and hopes for the future and wishes for things to be different.

And—

Being a soldier is the only thing I know how to be.

At least if I'm here, I know we're doing real work that's going to make a difference.

It's...fuck, but it's all I know how to do.

Perfume on a pillow. Dreaming about me. Stealing my cookies. Thinking about my smile and our time together.

It's all laid out there in black and white—why he felt like he had to leave, him thinking that doing that work is the only way he brings value.

And...

My sob is so strong it actually hurts.

Because I hate that he thinks that and I hate...that I was so scared of being left again of being hurt I pushed him away instead of stopping and realizing that the man I love is one who takes care of people, who's strong and determined to right the world's wrongs.

If I can't accept that about him then how can I truly say I *do* love him?

He's taken me as I come.

He's loved all the parts of me.

How can I not do the same for him?

But how can I accept that him being the man he is may mean that he'll leave us again and again and *again?*

I don't know.

I just...know I have to figure out a way.

———

I'm still no closer to an answer when Sunday dinner rolls around the next day.

I'm just gritting my teeth and forcing myself to believe I will find a way.

Banks is on the road, so he won't be here. But everyone else will be, including Lily, who's jetted over from a tour stop in Mexico.

I need to tell them what's happening.

Ask them to help me deal.

Because I'm done hiding from my family.

And I won't allow myself to push Colt away, even though I'm scared.

Now, if he would just make it home safe and sound so I could tell him that in person...

My eyes burn, but I just blink rapidly and put the roast into the oven, turn my focus to the mashed sweet potatoes and the salad I'm making to accompany it.

"Briar!" Dash calls. "We're here."

"And by *we*," Lily shouts, "he means all of us are about to invade."

I turn to see the *all of us* she's talking about and feel my lungs get tight as I see Frankie and Royal and Jade (they were on favorite aunt and uncle babysitting duties since I was "sick" the last two nights—a good thing considering my Sob Fest the previous evening). Atlas and Lily are on their heels, Atlas carrying Maisie in her car seat. Aspen and Willow are side by side, Dash trailing them, the diaper bag over his shoulder.

God, I love them.

Dash frowns. "Where's Colt?"

I exhale, prepare to tell them everything. "He's gone."

Dash's eyes flash and he opens his mouth, but it's not his voice I hear saying, "No, baby, I'm right here."

Thirty-Eight

Colt

One look at Briar's face and I know she's had a rough week.

And it's my fucking fault.

But that ends now.

"I'm here, baby," I say, reaching for her and yanking her into my chest. She melts against me at first but then gently pushes at me.

"Daddy!" Frankie's voice is filled with excitement, and she vaults herself into my arms the moment I turn.

"Hey, tater tot. Did you miss me?" I lift her up and spin her around.

Her eyes dance with delight. "I did! But you *said* you weren't leaving again!"

"I'll never leave you forever, but sometimes I have to work or travel. It's a grown-up thing."

"I don't like when you travel," she whispers.

"I know, but I'll always come back." I pop a kiss on the tip of her nose as I meet Briar's eyes.

She's upset, and I can't let this fester.

"How about you help get dinner going while Mommy and I talk for a minute?" I say, putting her down.

She frowns. "You're not going to do that thing where you take your pants off, are you?"

Jade presses a towel against her face to keep from laughing, and Willow hides hers in Dash's back. Even Briar has a half-smile going, so I take the opportunity to grab her hand and tug her out of the room.

"What the—" Dash yells out.

"Give us five minutes!" I call over my shoulder.

"Colt, what are you doing?" Briar asks in a heated whisper.

"We have to talk."

"I know, but this isn't—"

"Shh." I press a finger to her lips. "I don't want to fight. I need you to listen to me." We stop in front of the guest room. "Stay right here, okay? Give me ten seconds." I walk into the bathroom and dig the ring out of the back of the cabinet where I hid it. I take the ring out of the box, stuff it in my pocket, and then join her again in the hallway.

"Colt." Her eyes are filled with confusion, and I hate that I've done this to her—*again*—but it's truly the last time. I just have to make her believe it.

"Listen to me." I put my hands on either side of her face. "I love you and I am never leaving you. Do you hear me? Never, ever."

She blinks, more composed now.

But I'm not giving her a chance to dump me.

"Colt, I have to tell you—"

"Let me finish. Please." I hope she can see how important this is. "I'm back, just like I promised. I explained to you about Igor. This was a one-off and there won't be any more. There were some mini-missions toward the end of training, but I only really ever went on the one—the one where I was captured. Igor, who was my friend long before Russia, got me out. That's it. There are no more debts of honor or any other loose ends. All that matters now is us. You, me, and our family. Do you understand?"

She's gazing up at me, her expression filled with love and... understanding. I see it in her composure, her body language, and most of all—in her gorgeous green eyes. "I do and—"

"Do you want the good news or the bad news?" I interrupt because the damn ring is burning a hole in my pocket.

She almost seems amused as she says, "Surprise me."

"The good news is—I finalized all the paperwork, so I am officially out. Done. Finished." I watch her face, spotting the first hint of a smile, before continuing. "The bad news"—I pull out the ring and slip it on the fourth finger of her left hand—"is that your fiancé is an unemployed freeloader."

Her mouth opens but she doesn't make a sound as she stares down at the ring.

For the first time ever, I think I've shocked her speechless.

Then her gaze sharpens, and she arches her brows. "Well, *my* good news is—" She holds up her left hand. "—the answer is yes. But the bad news is that you better figure out what you're going to do for work because newborns are *expensive*."

"Newborns? Frankie's almost five."

She doesn't reply, merely stands there watching me watch her.

"Babe, are you saying...oh shit!"

Everything suddenly snaps into place and excitement fills me. She's pregnant!

Hot damn, she's pregnant. Again.

There must be some magic that happens when I'm inside her because we're basically two for two.

"Are you in for this, Colt?" she whispers, as if suddenly worried.

Yeah, that's not the mood I'm going for.

"Baby, I was *always* in. For anything and everything." Then I crush my mouth to hers, kissing her like I was just gone another four years instead of a week.

"*Colt.*" She's breathless when we finally pull apart and I press her against the wall.

"I'm right here, baby. For you, for Frankie, and for any other little ones who come along. I love you, Briar. More than fucking anything. I can't say I'll never spend another night without you, because life with me is always going to be an adventure—but you'll be at my side and in my life until I take my last breath."

"When did you buy me the ring?" she asks softly, putting her left hand against my shoulder.

"The day I found out about Igor. I was going to plan something special and then..." I shake my head. "I'm sorry the big romantic event I was trying to put together kind of fell by the wayside. But I'll make it up to you."

She laughs, but it's a soft, patient sound. "I don't need grand gestures, Colt. I just need to know you're coming home to me."

"Always."

"I was afraid history was repeating itself," she admits.

"You already knew about the baby?"

"I'd just found out. I came home early to tell you and... you were walking out the door."

"Dammit." I press my forehead to hers. "Better communication on both our parts going forward. Okay? Promise?"

She nods.

"Are you still mad?"

"No. I was never mad, just hurt. But then—" She pauses. "I read the letters, Colt. While you were gone."

The *letters*.

I'd forgotten about those.

"I think I understand you better now. The man you are." She curls her hand around my shirt, making sure she has my attention. "And just so you know, you are *so* much more than a soldier. You know that, don't you?"

"I don't know what I am," I say quietly. "All I know is that I love you."

"You're strong and brave and beautiful."

Our foreheads are still pressed together, and she's staring deep into my eyes.

"Colt?"

"I don't think...anyone's ever called me...beautiful before."

"But you are. Inside and out. A beautiful human being with a big, beautiful heart. Who wants to right all the wrongs in the world, one bad guy at a time. That's the man I fell in love with, so how can I love you the way I do and simultaneously ask you to be someone else?"

"I'm never going back to that life," I say firmly.

"That specific life, no. You can't. Not if you want to be Frankie's daddy—and daddy to this new little one." She takes one of my hands and presses it against her stomach. "But you have to be who you are, and we both know you need to be fighting off bad guys, one way or another. When you say life with you will be an adventure—I feel that in my soul. That's partly why I love you so much. Life with you *is* an adventure. The best kind of adventure."

"Yeah?" I pull in a deep breath. "I never want to hurt you again, Briar."

"You won't, as long as you're honest. We both probably need to stop having knee-jerk reactions to everything." She pauses. "And I do understand why you had to go get Igor. Is he okay?"

"He will be. He's in rough shape, but we got to him in time."

"Was anyone else...hurt?"

"No. My buddy Grim has a couple of broken ribs but nothing he can't handle. We had a SEAL team with us, so that's always a bonus."

"I'll bet."

"Are you sure you're okay? Ready to go on the next big adventure with me?"

"Do you already have one in mind?"

"I do." I wiggle my eyebrows, and she laughs.

"I'm ready, Colton Blackwood. Whatever it is, I'm ready."

"Excellent." I take her hand and lead her back to the kitchen. "Hey, Atlas! Fire up that jet of yours—we're going to Vegas!"

"Wait, what?" She tugs my arm. "What are you talking about?"

"Show them your ring, baby." I grin. "We just got engaged, and I've waited too long for this—we're getting married. Today, tomorrow, but we're not waiting."

"You're getting married?" Frankie asks, staring at us.

"You're engaged!" Aspen says at the same time.

"I knew it!" Willow grins, clasping her hands together.

"Yay!" Jade squeals with delight.

"You're serious?" Atlas asks when the girls immediately start hugging both of us.

"About Vegas? Hell, yeah." I glance at Briar. "A Vegas wedding?"

"I don't care where—I just want to do it."

"We can't do it without Banks," Aspen says hurriedly. "I mean, he'll be heartbroken."

That gives me pause.

Because she's right—all the guys have to be there.

"All right, hold off on the jet until Banks is back in town." I slide my arm around Briar. "But we're engaged!"

"Daddy?" Frankie's soft voice penetrates that excited laughter and chatter in the kitchen, and I look down to see a somber expression on her little face.

"What's wrong, baby?" I drop to my haunches so we're eye level. "Don't you want Mommy and me to be married?"

"I don't...what does that mean?" she whispers.

"It means I'm going to love you and your mommy forever and ever and ever. I was going to anyway, but when we get married, it makes us an official family."

"Oh." She's thoughtful and then she wraps her arms around my neck. "I'm glad you're my daddy."

She has no idea how much that means to me.

"I'm the luckiest daddy in the world," I whisper against her hair.

Fuck.

I'm going to cry again.

But that's okay—because they're happy tears.

I've got everything I ever wanted. And more.

Briar. Frankie. Another baby on the way.

And my brothers. Who've also met the women who make their lives whole.

It doesn't get any better than this. Hell, right now I can't think of a single adventure or mission better than the one I'm living right now.

This is what makes life worth living. Everything else? It's just background noise.

"Why are you guys whispering?" Briar asks, dropping down to our level, her eyes searching both of our faces.

"I was just explaining to Frankie what it means that we're getting married," I say.

"Can I get a new dress?" Frankie asks her mother.

"Yes, you can." Briar grins. "All of us girls are getting new dresses. And your uncles are going to wear tuxedos."

Frankie's eyes round. "Uncle Atlas only wears those to the stuffy parties," she stage whispers.

"And weddings," I say with a laugh.

I get to my feet and scoop her up, holding out a hand to Briar. She takes it and leans into my side.

"So, what's for dinner?" I ask.

"Wedding planning!" Willow and Jade say in unison.

Dash groans but there's a smile on his face as he meets my gaze across the room.

"Thank you," he mouths.

I should be thanking him for knocking me on my ass that first day of practice in Boston all those years ago. If he hadn't, I wouldn't be here now. None of us would.

That was the very first adventure.

I look around the room with an appreciative smile.

More than a decade later, the Gamebreakers are still going strong. Still brothers. Still a family.

Now there's just twice as many of us.

And I can't think of anything better.

EPILOGUE

BRIAR

My feet are killing me but the shoes I found on our day-long shopping spree are freaking gorgeous.

Cream-colored satin pumps with crystals embedded all throughout.

And they pair perfectly with the dress I found—or really, the dress that Jade, Aspen, Lily, and Willow found during our wedding planning extravaganza that was two nights ago.

Because Banks is playing here in Vegas tomorrow night.

So, he and the team flew in late last night after their game, and when he woke up, he joined Colt and the guys when they went off to get the marriage license and tuxes from Atlas's tailor.

Luckily, the Vipers' head coach was nice enough to let him out of the morning skate.

I smooth my hands down the front of the dress my new sisters found.

It's...perfect.

Everything I never thought I would have, but secretly wanted so, so badly.

I look like a princess.

The thin crystal-studded straps settle perfectly on my shoulders, but they don't dig in. They're supported by a corset that looks sheer in my torso but is actually lined with skin-colored mesh so I'm not exposed, and the bodice is lined in white. And the whole thing is covered with lace and crystals and pearls.

And don't even get me started on the skirt.

It's big and flouncy, miles and miles of organza that feels light enough to walk in but is adorned with those crystals and pearls and also a swathe of fabric flowers. And it has a high slit that makes me feel sexy, showing off plenty of leg.

Enough that Dash will be scowling as he walks me down the aisle.

And Colt will be drooling.

Total sexy princess, as Lily had called it when she showed me the laptop screen a couple of nights ago.

And kismet because the designer lives in L.A.

Loves Lily and Jade's music (and Willow's movies) and really, it pays to have friends in powerful positions.

Within twenty-hours I had a dress in my size and alterations underway.

And now I'm wearing it...and Frankie is wearing the matching one the designer made for her too.

And her shoes have sparkles too.

And my girls are dressed to the nines as well—gorgeous beyond measure, but it's not just the heels and dresses and hair and makeup we all had done.

It's that they're overjoyed for me. For Frankie. For Colt.

For the family we're building.

For all the joy that's coming our way.

My heart is full.

Because I'm happier than I ever thought possible.

There's a knock at the door, and Willow opens it.

"Is it safe to infiltrate the female zone?" Dash teases as he walks into the bridal room at the chapel, his hand over his eyes.

Willow huffs out a sigh and pulls his hand free. "It's safe, goofball."

He touches her cheek then turns my way and freezes, his face going soft in a way I've never seen before. Then he's striding over to me, his eyes damp, his voice a little rough. "You look beautiful, sis."

"Thanks, big bro," I whisper.

He hugs me carefully, mouth at my ear when he murmurs. "Like a fucking princess, Thorny. And I can't imagine anyone better than you to marry my best friend." He leans back, cups my jaw. "And I can't imagine anyone better to marry my sister than Colt."

There's a sniff.

And my eyes aren't dry either.

"No tears!" Aspen commands. "The makeup artist left already."

I suck in a breath, exhale—and I'm not the only one.

Then I have to do it again when he reaches his hand into his pocket and pulls out two boxes.

"From Colt," he murmurs, passing one to me and one to Frankie.

Inside are matching delicate gold bracelets with our initials on them.

Perfect.

Simple.

As is the letter Dash hands me.

> *I'll be the one waiting at the end of the aisle.*
> *-C*
> *P.S. I love you more than my next breath.*

We make it through the letters and the bracelets and the last minute preparations without having to do massive makeup repairs—though I do wipe away a tear when Dash crouches in front of Frankie and uses his big hands to carefully put on her bracelet.

Then the girls are walking out the door.

I smooth Frankie's hair back.

"You ready, baby?"

She nods vigorously, sending the bow in her hair shaking. "I'm ready!"

I grin, knowing our family is finally complete and watch her skip through the door.

"What about you?" Dash asks. "You ready?"

I nod. "More than ready."

"Good." He holds out his arm for me to take it. "Though, I'll still kill him if he hurts you."

Laughter bubbles up in my chest. "I love you, big bro."

"I love you too, Thorny."

We walk out into the chapel, and I see them, my family, all around.

The dream.

The fantasy.

My reality.

Jade is starting to show, but is still beautiful in her dress, Frankie standing at her side.

And Royal is next to her, holding my daughter's hand in the one that was so badly injured, the one that he wouldn't let her touch all that long ago. But he's been working hard at physical therapy, and he's coming along so well that he's working on a solo album.

Banks is in the opposite row, Maisie cradled against his chest. He looks as happy as I feel, and I know it's not because he's the league's leading scorer. It's Aspen, who's working on opening a second location for the Sapphire Room, and it's Maisie and...it's Mrs. X, who's here and all dolled up. She winks at me as Dash, and I pause at the end of the aisle.

My gaze swings back to the other side, seeing Lily and Atlas standing there. Lily is getting ready for a break before the

European leg of her tour, and no surprise, Atlas took over their wedding planning. So far there are four ceremonies in four different countries so the whole world knows she belongs to him. Lily laughed when she heard the news, patting his cheek and murmuring something in his ear that had him blushing.

God, I love him.

And I love them *together*.

Willow, beside them, just wrapped on her first movie since breaking free of her asshole of an ex and is positively radiant as she smiles at me.

Not merely pieced back together.

Whole and living a bright, beautiful life.

Because of the man beside me.

The music changes, but I don't start walking, even when Dash does.

He pauses, glances down at me. "Briar?"

I touch his cheek. "You know how much I love you, right?"

His eyes go damp. "You know I love you that much back, right?"

I nod.

He exhales, blinks, then smiles his patented Dash grin. "Then let's do this."

"Let's do it."

And then I take my first step toward forever.

Or maybe I'm already there.

———

WEST

A mariachi band is playing at full volume in my head, and the pounding is so loud I'm tempted to put my hands over my ears.

Fuck.

Last night might have been a bridge too far in Project I'm-getting-over-Briar-one-puck-bunny-at-a-time. Well, one specific puck bunny and way too many shots of tequila. That was a colossal mistake but one I've been making regularly the last few weeks.

All while watching the woman I fell in love with fall back in love with her ex.

I let her go without a fuss because, really—he had her first. He left her, and their baby, but that's a long sob story and I'm all out of fucks to give when it comes to him. The thing is, Briar went through enough while Colt was gone. She didn't need me to make her feel bad about going back to the love of her life. Who also happens to be her daughter's father.

Even if he left her for five fucking years.

But there's a lot of history between them, so I was never going to win that competition.

The old adage that nice guys always finish last? Yeah, I should consider getting that tattooed on my forehead.

After last night's shenanigans, I'm running late, so I practically skid into the dressing room to get out of my street clothes and into my gear.

"Someone looks rode hard and put away wet," my friend and teammate, Magnus, chirps.

I flip him the bird as I yank on my equipment.

Why does hockey require so many damn pieces? If I was an accountant, I'd already be sitting at my desk.

Despite the pounding in my skull and the bile threatening to come back up, I almost laugh at the thought of being an accountant. Numbers are definitely not my jam.

I sink onto the bench in the locker room and stuff my feet into my skates. Beside me, Banks is taping his stick.

"How's it going?" he asks.

"Good." We're close, but there's been a bit of distance between us since this thing with Briar. He introduced us, after all.

"You, uh, hear about the wedding?"

"Yup."

Briar married her ex the day before yesterday and of course, I forgot we were still friends on social media. Those pictures popped up and fueled my tequila-laden night of revelry.

"Dude, come on. It's me."

"Your loyalty is to Briar," I say quietly, focusing on lacing my skates. "I don't expect you to pick sides."

"It's not about *sides*," he says. "You're my friend too. You've been part of my life the whole time Colt was gone. I'm not going to walk away from all my other friends just because he's back."

"Doesn't matter anyway." I glance around since I don't want word to get out just yet, but I don't mind telling Banks. "I let my agent know that I'm interested in the new team in Atlanta. I'm down to be picked up in the expansion draft."

Banks just stares at me. "Is that really what you want? We're a family here."

I lift one shoulder in a shrug. "*You* have a family, Banks. I have teammates. Some friends. This isn't home to me. Management is good to us but it's common knowledge that you have a no-trade clause, so you're not going anywhere. That means Briar and Colt are going to be here. At the games. In the family lounge. Most team events...and I'm only human, man. I let her go without making a big deal because I know what she went through, but she hurt me. Watching her with him at every game—I can't do it."

A look of regret crosses his face, but then he nods. "I understand. I'm sorry it went down this way."

"This isn't on you. You had no way of knowing he would come back from the dead." I shake my head. "None of us did, least of all her."

We're both quiet for a beat.

What else is there to say? This isn't Banks's fault. It's not even Briar's, though she could have picked me. She could have—

Knock it off, McGregor.

That ship has sailed off into the sunset.

And left me on the shore.

"Anyway, I think if I offer myself up in the draft, that saves someone who really wants to stay. And a change of pace will do me good."

"There's all kinds of talk about the new franchise," Banks says thoughtfully. "Personal issues aside, there's a lot of money going into that team. It might become a great place to play."

"That's the plan." I give him a grin. "Anyway, keep this between us, okay? Right now, everything is on the down low."

"Absolutely." He cocks his head, squinting slightly, one side of his mouth quirking up. "You look like shit, by the way."

"Maybe." I chuckle. "But there was a lovely lady and a whole lot of tequila."

He grimaces. "You're a better man than me—I don't think I'd be here after a night of tequila."

"You must be getting old," I joke.

"Probably." He laughs and gets to his feet. "See you out there."

I nod and grab my gloves.

Time to focus on hockey because my days here are numbered.

If Atlanta doesn't take me, my agent knows I want to be traded.

Briar and Southern California are going to be in the past by summer.

And maybe by then, so will my broken heart.

———

Thank you for reading! We hope you loved Briar and Colt's book as we enjoyed writing it! This concludes the Gamebreakers series. Thanks for coming on this awesome ride with us!

And don't miss West's story in CHASING LOVE. **Sometimes heartbreak is just the beginning of the right love story...**

GAMEBREAKERS

ABOUT THE AUTHORS

USA Today bestselling author, Elise Faber, loves chocolate, Star Wars, Harry Potter, and hockey (the order depending on the day and how well her team — the Sharks! — are playing). She and her husband also play as much hockey as they can squeeze into their schedules, so much so that their typical date night is spent on the ice. Elise is the mom to two exuberant boys and lives in Northern California. Connect with her in her Facebook group, the Fabinators or find more information about her books at www.elise-faber.com.

facebook.com/elisefaberauthor

amazon.com/author/elisefaber

bookbub.com/profile/elise-faber

instagram.com/elisefaber

tiktok.com/@elisefaberauthor

goodreads.com/elisefaber

patreon.com/EliseFaber

About the Authors

USA Today Bestselling author Kat Mizera was born in Miami Beach with a healthy dose of wanderlust. She's lived from coast to coast, and everywhere in between, but home is wherever her family is.

A devoted mom and wife to her wonderful and supportive husband (Kevin) and two amazing boys (Nick and Max), Kat loves to travel the globe with her adventurous, hockey loving family. Greece is at the top of that list. She hopes to one day retire there, spending her days writing books on the beach.

Kat is former freelance sports writer who now writes steamy hockey romance about her favorite fictional teams, the Las Vegas Sidewinders and the Alaska Blizzard. The library of novels she's penned also include sexy contemporary stories about baseball stars, alpha sex club owners, special forces heroes, rock stars and royalty. Regardless of genre, her books about bad boys with hearts of gold will steal your breath, rock your world and melt your heart.

WHERE TO FOLLOW KAT:
www.katmizera.com
Kat's Private Facebook Group
https://bit.ly/KatMizeraFBGroup

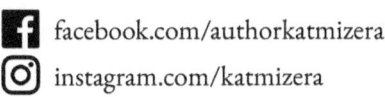

facebook.com/authorkatmizera
instagram.com/katmizera

www.ingramcontent.com/pod-product-compliance
Lightning Source LLC
Chambersburg PA
CBHW020058030726
47498CB00006B/1840